AF421398

CHERRY KILLS
SEAN THOMAS MCDONNELL

TINY WORLDS

First Edition
ISBN (print): 979-8-9924626-9-2
ISBN (ebook): 979-8-9941869-0-9

Published by Tiny Worlds Publishing
tinyworldspublishing.com

Cover Illustration by Butcher Billy
Cover & Interior Design by Shane Bzdok
Edited by S.E. Reid

Tiny Worlds Publishing and the Tiny Worlds
logo are trademarks of Tiny Worlds, LLC.

Tiny Worlds, LLC
2108 N ST # 8673
Sacramento, CA 95816
tinyworldspublishing.com

R3

WORLDS WORTH

DISCOVERING

tinyworldspublishing.com

For Quinn and Cian, my world.

* * *

CHAPTER ONE

NORMAL BRAINS

herry poked at her seared tofu and thought of her dad's face. It too was seared, but not with clean black lines. Not finished with a ponzu glaze. His face was a charred mask of nightmares. It blistered, melted. Always.

Although in her dream—the one that tormented her most nights for the past seven years—his face was calm, and his expression was one she'd never seen while he was alive. It was an expression that said, *Don't cry for me, Cherry. Everything is A-okay.* But then his face would melt, and the symbol, materializing, splitting the flesh on his forehead, would make her feel as if she were falling off a cliff. She'd wake up and push her thumbs into her eyes until blinding lights popped in her optic nerves. It obscured the image, but never for long enough. The glyph was always there, like the trailing light of a sparkler. Even now she could see the delicate flourishes of gold making up the intricate wings of the falcon, and the circle on top, its ever-watching eye at the center.

"Oh, Cherry. Always deep in thought." Ramon filled Cherry's water glass, removed a towel from his shoulder, and dabbed at the tablecloth. "You've hardly taken three bites. No good?"

"I'm just thinking about the economy, Ramon." Cherry smirked. "You think I'd just sit here if it wasn't any good? I'd give you shit—you know this."

She cut her tofu with the side of her fork and took a bite. "It's terrible. I'll sue."

"And here I thought you liked my cooking."

"I love your food, Ramon. Nobody knows my palate like you. That's why I'm going to sue you. I'm going to own this restaurant—then I'll be able to boss you around every night."

"You already boss me around." Ramon winked, then leaned in and whispered, "Would you like a brownie?"

"To go, if you don't mind." Cherry smiled and added, "Maybe I won't sue you after all."

Cherry couldn't afford to eat out every night, but that didn't stop her. After all, that's what credit was for, wasn't it? She'd told her case worker it was aspirational, motivation to live a quality life. She left out that she had never expected to live long enough to worry much about repayment. But now, at twenty-two years old, she'd come to the realization she would need to start living like someone with a future. Not a great future, but a future nonetheless. And while that might have been a comfort to most people, to Cherry it just seemed like a lot of work. It meant searching for a job—one that didn't make her feel like jumping off a bridge. But those gigs were for people with diplomas, ambition, and let's face it: normal brains.

If it weren't for Ramon and his restaurant, Cherry wasn't sure she'd have survived the past few years. He was the closest thing to a real friend she had, which would have been depressing if she had a moment to herself to think about it. But Uncle and the gang made sure that wasn't the case. That's why she'd snuck out—to pretend life wasn't so messy.

Black Garlic was a clean enough restaurant with decent food, but despite this, it was never crowded. Cherry liked it that way. It was private enough to keep her from feeling overwhelmed, public enough for her to remain part of the living world. Being at the apartment too much made her feel…absent.

The first time she'd come into Black Garlic, Ramon didn't pay her much mind, just the normal, *"How do you do?"* and *"Would you like pepper?"* and *"Ma'am, please remove your feet from the seat of that booth."* But as with all relationships built from duration more than commonality, eventually the notches lined up with the pegs, and although the relationship would never work outside the confines of the restaurant, within it the two ebbed and flowed as a single body of ponzu.

In a booth directly behind her, a woman whimpered. Cherry pretended to search for something in her bag to get a better look. She recognized the woman right away, with her glossy pink bangs pinned down by a sparkly barrette with a purple cat on it, hair that had always reminded Cherry of cotton candy.

Cherry touched her own hair, dry and fried from the at-home bleach job, a failed attempt to look like Debbie Harry. Uncle said she looked more like Daryl Hannah in *Blade Runner*.

The pink-haired woman was a regular at Black Garlic the past few months, always alone, always reading books at the back of the restaurant. They'd never spoken, just a head nod here and there, an acknowledgment of subculture, though what subculture didn't matter; it was an other recognizing an other—two cursive letters in a print world.

Black droplets from the woman's mascara trailed down her cheeks—leaving watercolor branches that fed directly into heavily-applied black lipstick—so that her eyes and mouth seemed connected by a stream of despair.

"Excuse me?" said the woman.

Cherry looked down at her tofu, pretending not to hear.

"Excuse me? Sorry to bother you—do you have a tissue?"

Cherry retrieved a tissue from her bag and handed it to the woman without saying a word. Cherry didn't want the world to suffer—even if she thought maybe the world deserved it a little— but this woman wanted more than a tissue. She could feel it in the woman's gaze. Charity wasn't her thing, the giving or receiving of it, which was one of the many reasons she'd snuck off to be alone tonight, to get away from the nagging, overprotective enclave of *Alternates* back at her apartment, always trying to save her. And fix her. Still, there was something about the woman's eyes, absent, searching for something in her mind, that made Cherry pause; they reminded her of her own eyes the night the detectives told her that her dad was dead, like she didn't already know.

Cherry signaled to Ramon, who came over in a hurry.

"Bring the lady a shot of that stuff you gave me last Friday," said Cherry. "Better make it a double." Then added, "Better go ahead and bring me one, too. Make mine a triple."

Ramon dashed off to retrieve the drinks.

The woman walked over to Cherry's booth, plopped down on the seat, and extended her hand. "Name's Mai."

Cherry gathered her belongings, pretending not to see Mai's hand. The woman seemed perfectly nice, but Cherry needed space—one night alone, for Christ's sake. She glanced at Mai and noticed her hands were blue. She was on the verge of yelling to Ramon to call for an ambulance, but then she saw the same blue on the woman's white boots. It was paint. "So what, you an artist?"

Mai nodded absently.

"I've always wished I could paint," said Cherry, "but every time I try, it's the same painting, a white dog in the snow. My problem...well, besides the talent thing...is coming up with a good idea. How do you come up with your ideas?"

Mai's eyes focused as if she'd returned from whatever horrible memory had tethered her to her sadness, and although the pain still lingered in the corners of her mouth and eyes, she managed a quiet reply.

"They hide from us until we've given up. But they'll find you, once you've stopped searching."

"Who will find us?" asked Cherry, pulling out a compact and reapplying the new candy-red lipstick she'd swiped from the Thrifty's on Main.

Mai's eyes widened in momentary panic.

"Whoa, hey, it's okay, honey," said Cherry, noticing the fear sweeping over Mai's face. "Whatever it is, you're safe here. Tell me what happened—someone mess with you? Tell me where they're at. I'll beat their ass. I will. I took a free Krav Maga class down at the Y a year ago, learned the best move is still a swift kick to the nuts. Some things never change I guess, you know?"

Ramon set the glasses on the table and patted Cherry's shoulder, then walked over to seat a couple well into a celebration. Cherry thanked God she wasn't a waitress, then remembered she was nearly broke and that maybe being a waitress had some perks, money being one of them. The supplemental checks from Uncle Sam only went so far.

Mai took Cherry's hand and squeezed. "I don't know what to do," she said in a desperate whisper. "It was real. It was real...it was...." She searched Cherry's face for confirmation that it was indeed real.

Cherry pulled her hand back.

She thought back to that night at the apartment, Elwood coming out of the flames to save her from the smoke and fire, carrying her out into the fresh night air. That wasn't real. Psychosis, the doctor had said. But, psychosis or not, it wasn't going away anytime soon, so she'd learned to accept it, but to keep it hidden. It wasn't real, but it sure felt like it.

Cherry retrieved her eyeliner and pulled her lid down to apply it. Her caseworker told her to go easy on the makeup while she looked for a job, but any employer who didn't respect a Cleopatra eye inspired by the great Vivien Leigh, or high-arched brow inspired by Claudette Colbert, was not a good fit. Also, fuck them.

"Okay, sure. I believe you," said Cherry. "It was real. Who am I to say what's real and what isn't anyway? I'm the worst person to make that call, truly. Here, sip this."

Mai downed her drink, then reached for Cherry's glass and sipped.

"Okay…" said Cherry. "Well, I probably would have gotten shit from Uncle if I came home loopy anyway."

Mai didn't seem to notice this comment. Her eyes were still far away. Then she spoke, "Have you ever been to the Gut Punch?"

Cherry put her makeup back in her bag, took the cigarette from behind her ear, and placed it beneath her nose. She didn't smoke, but she liked the smell of cigarettes, and she liked to hold them and let them hang from the corner of her mouth, just like her dad used to.

"Little punk bar a few blocks from here, right?" Cherry asked.

Mai sank into her seat and looked around nervously.

"It's alive," she said, her eyes welling with fresh tears. "It knew me."

"It knew you?" Cherry said, matching Mai's whisper. "What do you mean it knew you? *Who* knew you?"

"I don't know how to explain it." Mai's lip quivered as she spoke. "It...you know that feeling you get when walking alone at night? Or when you're passing by an open closet door...it's that feeling that something's there—something that can get you. It's an old fear. Like it's always been a part of us."

"Yes. I know what you mean. Seems like there's always something at my heels."

Mai continued, "Well, the Gut Punch has always been a sanctuary for me. Best tots in the City, too." She smiled briefly. "But, today it was different."

"Different, how?"

"It's hard to explain without sounding like a nut job. They'd hired me to paint a mural on the wall in the back room, a giant squid fighting a whale. Everything was going fine—some of my best work. Then I felt that feeling, like someone was behind me. I looked, but nobody was there, so I kept going. Then...."

Cherry moved in closer. "Go on."

"The squid's eye opened. I thought I was imagining it. Maybe I was too focused—like my eyes were fatigued, you know? But then I felt its tentacle arm weaving between my legs. I screamed, but when the owner came running back to help me, the painting was back on the wall. It was just a painting."

"Interesting," said Cherry, leaning back in her seat.

"You don't believe me?"

"I believe you think you saw what you saw. The mind is tricky—trust me on that one."

"Well, I have proof," said Mai, standing and hiking up her skirt. There on her thigh was a puckered, circular red mark, and a deep bruise in the shape of a snake climbing her leg.

"Shit," said Cherry. "Well, that's more than tired eyes or an overactive mind."

"I ran out of that place without even getting paid. I didn't even grab my bag! My portfolio, wallet—everything was in there!"

"Christ, well…"

"Could you go get it for me?" Mai said, a glimmer of hope in her eyes. "I know it's a lot to ask, but I can't go back…"

Cherry tucked the cigarette behind her ear, took the glass from Mai's hand, and downed the brown liquid. "Sorry, no can do. Have to get home or Uncle is gonna be pissed. Maybe you can call them up, have them hold it for you until tomorrow.

Or ship it—"

Mai sobbed.

Cherry wasn't lying about needing to get back home. Uncle had probably already discovered she was missing, and when Uncky got angry, the walls shook. But more than that, she just wanted a moment of independence to prove she could handle life on her own, even if she wasn't sure this was entirely true.

Still, Mai seemed a good egg, and whatever had happened to her at the club really shook her up. Besides, wasn't everyone always calling her apathetic? Telling her to care more about things? Well, maybe she'd start here, with Mai. A quick way to prove to her messy brain she didn't need any help from these hallucinations—not anymore. A way to prove she could not only take care of herself, but also other people, and that she wasn't completely broken.

Cherry looked at Ramon, who shrugged.

"Listen, I can't stand to see a lady crying. I'll go—I'll go!" Cherry stood and headed toward the door. "I'm curious about these tots anyway. They're on you, by the way."

"Thank you! Thank you so, so much! What's your name?"

Cherry turned to face Mai. "Cherry Kills."

Mai's eyes widened. "Is that short for something?"

"Cherilyn," said Cherry, then threw out a peace sign and walked out the door.

* * * NORMAL BRAINS * * *

CHAPTER TWO

NOBODY HERE BUT US CHICKENS

herry rolled her shoulders. The conversation with Mai at Black Garlic made her tense. She was always tense interacting with other people.

Much like the restaurant, downtown wasn't crowded. It never was on weeknights. The hypnotic rhythm of her boots on the pavement, along with the ambient noise of distant traffic, relaxed Cherry. The City was hers, and she was the City's, at least for the moment. But as at home as she was, she couldn't help but feel a tinge of panic when she thought of what they'd say to her when they woke up to find her gone. *They're going to kill me.* She quickened her step and turned into the mouth of a darkened alley, but paused.

Broken shipping pallets and garbage cluttered the narrow glistening strip. She covered her nose to dull the scent of motor oil and cabbage. A single streetlamp shone down into a cone at the end of the alley. It was the quickest way to the club, but she felt that familiar feeling: someone was watching her. Waiting for her. She shrugged it off and stepped into the dimly-lit alley.

Up ahead of her, a rat scurried across Cherry's path, and as her eyes followed the large rodent's break for a pile of black trash bags, a familiar figure appeared at the end of the alley. She couldn't see his face, but she recognized the man immediately from his ten-gallon gut, tree trunk arms and legs, and his hunched back that reminded Cherry of a gigantic, quill-less hedgehog. *Uncle.*

"Eff," said Cherry, turning to run in the opposite direction. But there at the other end was another silhouette, this one with long, furry ears. It hopped toward her.

She turned and saw the big man trundling down the alley from the other direction. She'd known the alley was risky, but what choice did she have? Downtown was made up of long, hilly blocks, and her boots weren't exactly in city-hike condition.

Then, from between two dumpsters, a delicate laugh. The whole crew was here.

"Okay, Daisy—come on out," said Cherry. "I know I've been caught."

A little girl in a yellow dress with orange flowers embroidered on the skirt came skipping from between the dumpsters, smiling like she'd just been given a slice of cake. White socks extended to the balls of her brown ankles from shiny patent leather shoes. Her curly black hair in pigtail braids were tied with colorful, glittery ball bands in three places.

"Hi, Mama," said the girl.

"Don't call me that—I'm not your Mama. What are you doing here?" Cherry said, watching Uncle lumber down the alley.

"We woke up and you were gone."

"I needed some alone time."

"We needed some Cherry time," said Daisy with a laugh. "Uncle is mad at you."

Cherry rolled her eyes and ran her hand through her bleached hair, separating strands of tangles.

"Uncle is always mad at me. Is Elwood upset?"

Daisy put her finger to her chin and looked up. "I'm not sure. I don't think so. His face always looks the same."

Uncle was breathing heavily as he approached. He wiped at his broad forehead with the bottom of his sleeveless white undershirt and frowned.

Elwood stood expressionless, his large white paw-hands at his side. Cherry used to think he was ridiculous, the most obvious signal that something in her brain snapped that night, but over the years she came to accept his presence more than the others; a silent friend is often the most appreciated.

"Well, here we are again," said Cherry, taking the cigarette from behind her ear and placing it beneath her nose. "Would it kill you guys to give me one night off?"

Uncle was still catching his breath, and Daisy was playing an impromptu game of hopscotch. Cherry looked at Elwood. "Well, Elwood? Are you pissed?"

Elwood wiggled his nose and shook his head.

"Thanks, Elwood."

"I just don't get it," Uncle said, leaning against the brick wall. "What the hell compels you to do these things? What if somethin' were to happen to you?"

"As I've told you, I can take care of myself. I don't

need a little girl, a grouchy lug, and a goddamn giant rabbit watching over me. You're not exactly the super team you think you are. I need to pick up something for a friend. Can I please just do this alone?"

"We'll come with you, Cupcake."

"Cupcake? Jesus, Uncle—you're a remnant of those bygone years, aren't you?"

"Maybe I am. Where we headin'? And since when do you got friends?"

"Do you remember that girl from Black Garlic with the pink hair? You said you thought you saw her smile at Daisy a few months ago, so we sent Dayz over to her table to find out, but she just kept reading her book. Then I made fun of you the rest of the night. You remember that?"

Uncle groaned. "I swear to Christ it looked like she could see her—so I was wrong, sue me."

"I would if I could, big man. Now, I hope you brought your dancing boots—we're going clubbing."

Uncle closed his eyes and pinched the bridge of his nose.

"Uncle, you're such a baby. Do you always need to be so—" Cherry's words were cut short as a man emerged from the shadows, rubbing his eyes like he'd just woken up.

"Hey, you okay?" said the man as he stumbled into the alley. He was wearing a clean but wrinkled tan trench coat. His hair was disheveled but groomed. His smile, expensive and sleazy.

"Fine," she said. "Just fine."

"Good. I thought I heard you talking to someone…?"

"Nobody here but us chickens." Cherry turned to go, but the man grabbed her arm.

Uncle stepped forward; Cherry shot him a glance that said *What are you going to do? He can't even see you.* Uncle grimaced but stayed back, pacing back and forth like an antagonized tiger, his square fists at his side.

"What's your name, honey?"

"Get your hands off me, chump!" Cherry lifted her knee into the stranger's groin.

The man moaned and fell to the ground, where he curled into a ball of agony.

"Touch the pussy, you're gonna get fucked! Asshole." Cherry snarled and brushed off her arm where the man had grabbed her.

Elwood hopped over and kicked at the ground with his large white feet, pretending to cover the man in dirt.

"Alright, everyone," said Cherry. "Let's go. And let's try not to make a scene, okay?"

"Touch the pussy and you're gonna get fucked?" Uncle shook his head. "What does that even mean?"

"I don't know. Heard someone say it at a show one time."

"Mama," said Daisy. "You have to put money in the swear jar."

"Am I able to prepay for more words?" Cherry

pretended to tug on Daisy's braid, her hand unable to grasp the imaginary hair. "And please, stop with the 'Mama' shit, okay?"

"That's another quarter, Mama."

CHAPTER THREE

SEVEN YEARS EARLIER

herry rummaged through her dad's
closet looking for his baseball
bat. She hated being alone in the
apartment at night. Dad was out 'at
the shop,' as he'd say. What shop that
was and what he did there was unclear.
Something having to do with antiques.
But Cherry knew when to ask questions
and when it was better to be left in
the dark about certain things. They
had a roof over their heads and food
on the table. Wasn't that more than
some? She wrestled the chrome baseball
bat from a curtain of dangling coats
and shirts, and immediately felt better
having the Louisville Slugger in her
hands. As she closed the door, she
spotted a box on the top shelf of the
closet where her dad kept his hats.
It was too high to reach. She moved a
chair in from the kitchen, climbed up,
and took down the box.

It was the size of a VCR and heavier than she'd
expected. She set the box on the shag carpet and
lifted the lid; her heart sank. Inside was a revolver
and an antique book. She picked up the gun which
was so heavy she was forced to use two hands,

and even then, the barrel was never completely horizontal. She set the revolver next to her on the carpet, looked down the hallway to ensure the coast was clear, and then carefully removed the book. It looked ancient. As if it would at any moment turn to dust in her hands. But she couldn't put it down. She was too enthralled by the foreign letters and symbols on the worn leather cover. She ran a hand over the words and felt...strange. Electric.

A photograph fell out from between its pages. Cherry picked it up and felt an avalanche of emotions. It was her mom at a party. Her smile was Cherry's smile. Her eyes, although brown and not blue, were Cherry's eyes. The only photo she'd ever seen of her mom was in her dad's bedside table. But this was a picture she'd never seen before.

A jangling came from the front door. It was her dad's keys.

She slid the photograph back into the book and then set the book and revolver back into the box.

She'd just managed to put the box back on the shelf when her dad came into his room. Cherry was still standing on the chair.

"I was looking for a hat to wear," Cherry said with an awkward smile. "Would you mind if I borrowed one?"

"Cher, I don't want you in here while I'm out. You hear me?" Her dad frowned and helped her down from the chair. He shut the closet door and raised a brow. "And what are you doing with my bat?"

"Thinking about taking up the game." Cherry walked out to the living room with the bat slung over her shoulder. On the coffee table was a VHS tape.

Cherry snatched the case from the table and shouted, "What did you bring us?"

Her dad took a beer from the fridge and cracked it open. "Nothing you'd like."

"Wait—you got Jaws? Thank you! Thank you! Nothing scarier than ocean horror."

"That right? I'll order a pizza."

Cherry looked at her dad's eyes. They seemed distant.

"Dad?"

"Yeah Cher?"

Cherry paused, searching her dad's face for more evidence of…of what? "What do you do?"

"What do I do? What do you mean?"

"For a job. You work at a shop?"

"That's right. I work at a shop." Her dad wiped a line of condensation off the face of his beer with his pinky. "What do you want on your pizza?"

Cherry opened the VHS case, took out the tape, and inserted it into the VCR. She wasn't sure how far she wanted to take this conversation. Did she really want to know what her dad did for a living?

"What type of shop is it?"

"Well, we buy and sell antiques—nothing too exciting."

"Is it safe?" She said it before she could stop herself. A silly question—of course it was safe.

Cherry's dad put down his beer and looked into her eyes. "I'm a big dude, Dogstar. Nobody messes with me."

CHAPTER FOUR

GOTTA START SOMEWHERE

Daisy and Elwood played pat-a-cake while Uncle surveyed the area outside the club. Going on seven years, Cherry still felt an urge to apologize to the people around her for her *Alternates,* a term she'd given her little gang of imaginary friends. The doctor called them a "coping mechanism." Cherry couldn't see how a rabbit-man, an overprotective lug who reminded her of a cross between Henry Rollins and Ron Perlman, and a six-year-old girl who looked an awful lot like Ruby Bridges, could help her cope.

"The mind is a mysterious thing," the doctor had said.

Yeah, no shit, she thought.

The bouncer working the door of the Gut Punch wasn't particularly large, but what he lost in stature, he made up for in asshole. He looked from Cherry's face to her ID, then back again. "You should smile more."

"I am smiling," said Cherry, her face as expressionless as she could make it. "I hear you guys have killer tots, this true?"

"I don't eat tots—I ain't twelve years old."

"I didn't realize there was an age restriction on tots. There a band tonight?"

The bouncer took a flyer off the wall and handed it to Cherry. She read it aloud, "'Doomsday Snooze Button.' Sounds cheery. Do I have to pay the cover if I'm just coming in for a drink?" Cherry pulled out a five, her last bit of cash for at least a week until the next state-issued check came in, and handed it to the doorman. Then she uncapped her lipstick.

"You serious? Put your lipstick on *inside* the club." The bouncer waved a couple of tough-looking customers forward.

Cherry folded the flyer in half, blotted her lipstick with it, then handed the flyer back to the bouncer. "Thanks, it's been a pleasure. You remind me of my uncle—sweet as pie." Behind her, leaning against the brick wall of the club, Uncle grumbled.

The Gut Punch was already uncomfortably humid. The scent of stale beer and fried foods reminded Cherry of the apartment she shared with her dad when he was still alive; all it needed was Mingus playing on a chrome turntable and the occasional waft of reefer and she'd be right there in his living room, eating Cap'n Crunch out of the box on the shag carpet, watching *Cleopatra*.

Cherry posted up at the bar where a man with floppy orange hair and a bullring leaned in and said, "Love your earrings—that's an ankh, right?"

Cherry held up her hand to quiet Flop and shook her head. If there was one thing she couldn't stand, it was talking Egypt with creepers.

The opening band was only just sound-checking, the bass player plucking at the strings on his guitar and the drummer looking around for the nod from his bandmates to count them off.

Cherry waved down the bartender. "Give me whatever this guy *isn't* having, thanks. Maybe something vodka-y. Something with lime. You take credit, right?"

The bartender nodded and brought Cherry a drink, which she raised to Uncle and Elwood, who sat at a small table in the corner.

On the edge of the stage Daisy smiled while talking to herself, swinging her legs like a clock hand. The opening band nervously tightened and tuned their instruments, unaware of the happy-go-lucky imaginary little girl at their feet.

"My friend Mai left her bag here," Cherry said, turning back to the bartender. "She painted a mural out back or something. You mind if I grab it for her?"

The bartender raised her eyebrows. "That chick's your friend? She's an odd duck, isn't she?"

Cherry shrugged. "Well, if she's odd, I'm not sure where that leaves me. You have the bag or...?"

"In the back. Staff room, right next to the mural. Should be unlocked."

Flop leaned in. "I saw her leave in a hurry—she okay? I went back there, after she'd run out, thought maybe a dude was messing with her. Was gonna have some words with him, you know?" Flop pounded his fist on the bar top, almost spilling his beer.

"Do that again and you're out of here," said the bartender.

"Apologies—I just can't stand men who abuse women. I'm like Kurt that way."

Cherry rolled her eyes, paid her tab, and then walked to the back of the club. The sign on the door leading to the backroom read, "Renovation in Progress. Keep Out." Cherry opened the door and stepped into the room. It wasn't a large space, but big enough for a few standing tables and a low, vacant stage in the corner. It smelled like paint, mildew, and beer. She set her drink down on a small table beside the door and hugged herself. "Holy shit—it's colder than a dead penguin in here."

"That's a quarter, Mama," Daisy said, skipping into the room. Elwood hopped in behind her, wiggling his pink nose.

Uncle walked around the room, chest puffed out, lip curled; this was his no-nonsense look, which always made Cherry want to laugh—what could a figment of her imagination possibly do to protect her?

"How do you even know what a quarter is, Daisy?" Cherry shut the door behind them, then walked up to the mural. Mai was good, *really* good. Looking at the thrashing sperm whale being strangled by the giant pink squid, she could practically smell the briny sea air.

Daisy shrugged. "I don't know. Maybe because

we're you? Like the doctor said, we're hallu… hallusu—

"Hallucinations," Cherry said, bending slightly to look into the eye of the giant squid. The mural was bigger than she'd expected, the squid's eye the size of a dinner plate. She ran her hand over a tentacle arm, which stretched across the entire length of the room.

"What's that?" said Uncle, pointing to a symbol written in ink on the wall above the door to the staff room. "Looks a lot like that silly thing you're always doodling."

Daisy looked up to see what Uncle was talking about. "Hey, he's right. It's not the same, but sorta." She giggled.

Cherry stepped back; yes, it was a lot like the symbol in the fire of her dreams from the night everything fell apart. Like the glyphs in the book her dad kept hidden in the closet, right next to his gun. But this symbol didn't call to her like the one from her dream did. In her dream, the glyph burned her chest from the inside out. Just before she'd wake up, her dad always said the same thing: "Keep it a secret."

"Mama," said Daisy, "why is it glowing?"

Uncle stepped in front of Cherry. "Stay back!"

Cherry moved forward to get a better look. "Why do you have to be like this, Uncle? Sure, it's… strange…but that doesn't mean it's dangerous."

Elwood pointed a furry finger at the squid's eye.

"Eff," said Cherry, as the dinner plate eye darted

from Uncle to her.

Uncle put his fists up and shouted, "Cherry, run for the—"

The water collapsed, gushing into the room from where Mai had painted it onto the wall, and all at once Cherry was holding her breath, watching flyers, napkins, and chairs float by. The room was underwater.

Uncle swam toward her, a pale, enraged, tuskless walrus, but just as he was reaching out for Cherry's hand, a tentacle arm shot out and grabbed him from around his large waist, pulling the big man effortlessly to the opposite side of the room, away from her.

There was just enough space between the ceiling and the water for Cherry to swim to the surface and take a deep breath before being pulled back under. It had her leg, reeling her in like a thrashing, confused fish.

Daisy slapped at the squid's tentacle arm constricting Uncle, while Elwood rabbit-kicked its massive, gelatinous head.

It didn't make sense to Cherry; her Alternates were never able to interact with anything physical before. Yet here they were, tangled in the same violence she was. She thought maybe it wasn't real at all, that all this might be in her head, but then a tentacle arm punched her in the stomach, the blow so terrific Cherry thought the squid might have broken one of her ribs. She winced in pain.

A muffled yell—Cherry opened her eyes to see

a thousand bubbles ascend from Uncle's Alka-Seltzer shout as he tore the squid's sentient arm in half with his bare hands. Oil-black blood plumed from each end of the severed arm. Uncle's eyes brimmed with satisfaction. Finally free from the squid's grasp, he launched himself off of the squid's pink body toward Cherry.

Elwood motioned to Daisy, who in turn hooked a small arm around the rabbit-man's neck and swung onto his back as if he were a horse and she the star of a Wild West show. She stuck her head between his ears and bubble-shouted, "Yee haw!"

The squid evaded the whale, its gigantic eye momentarily pinning Cherry down in fright.

Cherry and Uncle swam toward the door. The giant squid darted after them, its head elongated by the tension force of its movement.

A tentacle latched onto Cherry's forearm, the pain from its suction cups intensifying by the second. With her free hand, she grasped at the door handle and, kicking the briney beast directly in its eye with her boot, managed to get just enough slack to open the door.

She slam-slid out of the fray and into the middle of the main room, gasping for air as ten punks who'd been drool-watching the opening band looked down at her with a mixture of annoyance and disinterest.

Cherry was soaking wet, but there wasn't an ocean in the room—none of the water had come out with her. She stood, raced to the door leading to the mural, and looked in. The room was trashed, and wet, but the ocean and squid were back on the wall. She leaned in to get a better look.

Uncle moved to block the door. "You nuts?"

"Based on what just happened, I'd say it's very likely." Cherry wiped the water from her face, then licked her lips. "Salt water?"

Daisy pointed to Cherry's arm. "Mama, are you okay?"

Cherry looked down at the circular mark on her arm. It was puffy and red, just below the hummingbird tattoo on her forearm. "It hurts worse than it looks. I guess this is the price we pay for altruism. Remind me to never do another good deed for as long as I live."

"Can we get the hell out of here now?" Uncle looked around the room with disgust. "Only thing worse than giant squids are opening bands."

"Gotta start somewhere," Cherry said, walking toward the exit.

"Oh, hey!" said the bartender. "Your friend's bag was behind the counter. Not sure how I missed it." She narrowed her eyes. "Why are you wet?"

Cherry felt like she was going to puke, but took the bag from the bartender's hand and shrugged. "Um...sweat? I'm a dancing machine."

EIGHT YEARS EARLIER

CHAPTER FIVE

herry pretended to read a book, covertly glancing up every few moments to watch her dad on the phone in the kitchen. He looked nervous, which wasn't normal for him; Mitch Kills could carry a cup of hot tea across a battlefield and never spill a drop. It wasn't exactly ice water in his veins—no one ever accused her dad of lacking passion—but he wasn't made of the same stuff as other men. Cherry wanted to be as brave as her dad, but her imagination didn't cooperate. But tonight, her dad's bravery seemed tentative.

She walked to the fridge and pretended to look for something to eat.

"I told you—it happens tonight," whispered her dad. "Ito's been cutting us out for too long. It's time." He wrapped the coiled phone cord around his knuckles and paced in small spurts across the length of the kitchen. "We won't get another chance." Her dad slammed the receiver to its base.

Cherry grabbed a Capri-Sun and went back to the couch in the living room.

"Everything okay?"

"Peachy. I'm going out tonight. Shop work."

Cherry didn't speak. She'd hoped she'd get used

to it, but she still felt like crying whenever her dad left her alone at night.

Her dad watched her from across the room. Gradually, his demeanor changed, and he said softly, "I got you something downtown, Dogstar." He left the room and came back with a small painting, no larger than a postcard. On it was a watercolor of a hummingbird with its long beak dipped into a delicate blossom.

Cherry wasn't sure what to say. It was pretty, sure, but she wasn't really a hummingbird type of girl. Maybe a vampire bat or a raven, but a hummingbird?

"It's nice, Dad. Thanks."

"I know it's not something you'd typically display in your room, so if you don't want to, that's okay. I just…they have big hearts."

"Who? Hummingbirds?"

"Yeah. Huge hearts. That's how they're able to move so fast. Anyway, I got this for you because you've got the biggest heart out of anyone I've ever met. I love you, baby. Never forget that."

That night, Cherry put the painting of the hummingbird into her sock drawer. Then she walked to the kitchen, pulled a knife from the knife-block, and placed it beneath her pillow. She slept with the lights on.

CHAPTER SIX

6666

CHAPTER SIX

ncle's silence on the walk back
to Black Garlic was deafening.
Cherry wanted him to yell at her,
to admonish her for getting them into
the mess back there at the club, but
his face was like stone as he lumbered
down the street.

Daisy was still on Elwood's shoulders, singing. *"But if I do, my mama will say, have you ever seen a squid squeeze, poor little Cherry, down by the bay."*

Cherry stopped walking and turned around to face her Alternates. "So…what the fuck happened back there?"

"You tell us, Cupcake." Uncle folded his thick arms. "You know what we was gettin' into?"

"Not really. I mean, sure, Mai said the squid came to life and—"

"So you knew this but didn't bother tellin' us?" Uncle let his arms fall to his side, his fists balled.

Daisy giggled. "I think Uncle's mad again."

Elwood put his hand up to cover Daisy's mouth.

"I thought she was…I don't know…having a hard night or something. If I had known we were going to be taking a swim, I wouldn't have worn my boots. They're all squishy now—"

"You're a dingbat, Cherry." Uncle unclenched his fists and headed in the direction of Black Garlic. Cherry, Elwood, and Daisy followed behind him. "Next time someone asks for help, if there's a giant squid, say no. It seems like a no-brainer to me."

"Okay, Uncle. The next time someone needs something, if they mention a squid, I'll ask them how big it is before I agree to help. But let's talk about how you ripped that thing's arm off. You've never been able to blow out a match, let alone make calamari."

"Don't know—maybe none of it happened. Maybe it's all in your head."

Cherry held up her throbbing red arm. "Then what's this?"

"You was tellin' us about the...um," Uncle scratched at his chin cleft, which was so pronounced it made him look like a cartoon pilot. "Oh, the stigmata. After watching that movie with the girl...she was the devil or somethin'." He snapped his fingers. *"The Exorcist."*

"That movie was scary," said Daisy, shaking her head.

"It was sick—why can't we ever watch a comedy? It's always horror or *Cleopatra*." The light was red, Uncle held out a hand to keep Cherry from crossing the street.

Cherry walked through Uncle's large hand as if he weren't there at all and crossed the street. "There aren't any cars coming. Can you just back off for a moment? Besides, we don't just watch *Cleopatra*, we watch *all* of the Cleopatras. You get something different with Liz Taylor, Claudette

Colbert—Vivien Goddamn Leigh!"

Uncle rolled his eyes and continued, "You said the stigmata can happen if you believe it. Like, your body can create a symbol or somethin', right?"

"Yeah, well, I'm a child of the eighties," said Cherry. "We know a lot about dumb shit like stigmata, possession, satanic cults—quicksand! But is any of it real? I mean, sure, people worship the Devil, but do they kidnap and sacrifice virgins?"

"Cherry," Uncle sighed and shook his head, "can you just focus for a moment?"

At Black Garlic, the booth where Mai had been sitting was empty. Cherry gave Ramon an inquisitive look from across the room, where he was folding napkins.

Ramon shrugged. "She left."

"Well, that's great," said Cherry under her breath. "We almost get murdered by a giant squid and she doesn't even stick around?"

"Should we look in her bag?" asked Daisy, climbing down from Elwood's back.

"I guess we'd better." Cherry unzipped the bag and rummaged through it. There were brushes, cans of acrylic and spray paint, palette knives, and rags. Within the side pocket of the bag was a photograph. It was a young Mai standing in front of a bungalow with an older man who looked like he might be her dad. Cherry flipped the picture over and read the back, "Cedar Street. 1985."

Daisy read the house number. "6666."

Uncle shook his head. "We ain't goin' there tonight, Cupcake. We're goin' home. In fact, we're never goin' there—not to a house with that number!"

Cherry shoved the photo back into the bag and zipped it up. "We'll go home, but I'm returning this bag to Mai tomorrow. And, just so you know, 6666 isn't the number of the beast. That's 666."

"It's six thousand times worse. We ain't goin', and that's final."

Daisy shook her head. "That doesn't sound right."

Cherry waved bye to Ramon and headed out the door. "You might be able to handle a giant squid, Uncle, but don't try me."

* * * 6666 * * *

NO MORE CRYING IN THE SHOWER

CHAPTER SEVEN

herry let the hot water run down
her face. She wondered how a brain
could be so terribly rewired from
a single event. The doctor said it was
trauma, and while Cherry certainly
didn't dispute she'd been traumatized,
it didn't explain the symbol burned
into her brain—and it didn't explain
the purple bruise on her forearm from
the *giant fucking squid* that popped off
the mural at the Gut Punch.

She wanted to stay in the shower longer, but she had a big day ahead of her. She needed to track down Mai to return her bag, and then she'd need to start the horrible task of finding a job.

"Knock knock. You okay in there?" A low voice came from outside in the hall.

"Jesus, Uncle! Can I have a little privacy?"

"Just wanted to make sure you're okay—don't have to bite my head off."

Cherry felt silly arguing with her Alternates, but as unreal as they were, they were too annoying to ignore.

She turned the hot water up until it was nearly scalding. She thought of her dad and how painful it must have been to be eaten by flames. She drew the symbol from her dream with her pinky finger in the condensation of the shower door; it was hard to get it just right. It looked a little like the mark on the wall at the Gut Punch.

She held back the tears. No more crying in the shower, she told herself.

As steam from the shower continued to fill the room, Cherry's mind drifted to a time before the fire. She welcomed it. She gave into the reverie.

"Cherry," her father said tapping on the glass of a large wooden display case, "your favorite piece." They were back at the Isis exhibit at the City Museum, eight years ago. One year before the fire. It was their Saturday ritual. Her dad would recount to Cherry some of his experiences while living in Egypt, and Cherry would laugh or gasp, depending on the tale. Her dad embellished, she was sure of it, but she never called him out on it. She didn't mind. She looked into the display case and saw the gold crown in the shape of a vulture. Two ruby eyes stared back at her.

She read the display plaque, "Vulture Crown of Isis." She looked at her dad. "You think anyone laughed at the bird on her head?"

Her dad smiled and scratched his scruffy cheek. "I don't think anyone laughs at a goddess. But she didn't take herself too seriously."

"You two buds back in Egypt or something?"

"Something like that," said her dad moving on to the next display case.

Cherry tried desperately to hold onto the memory—she wanted to run to her dad and hug him.

"Knock knock," said Uncle from outside the bathroom door.

Cherry ran her hand over the shower door glass, wiping the symbol away.

"I'm coming! Keep your imaginary pants on!"

THE CHERRY SHOW

CHAPTER EIGHT

On the bus out of the City, Cherry talked with her Alternates without feeling out of place, knowing that anyone who takes public transit expected at least one loner rambling to themselves.

When they got to 6666 Cedar Street, a brown bungalow with a tortoiseshell cat sitting in the driveway, Daisy pointed to the canary-yellow house next door. A woman peeked from behind a curtain at Cherry, who felt like a dead rose beneath her gaze. Across the street, a man mowing his lawn walked back and forth across the green grass with a scowl on his face.

"Mama, why are they looking at us like that?" Daisy frowned, hiding behind Cherry's leg.

"They're not looking at you, Daisy. They can't see you. They're looking at me because I'm disrupting their play." Cherry waved at the woman, who jerked the curtains closed.

"There's a play happening?" Daisy popped out from between Cherry's legs and looked around enthusiastically.

Uncle shook his head. "No, Dayz. What she means is that they like vanilla, and Cherry is Cherry."

"They're not used to seeing so much style in suburbia." Cherry covered her mouth as she spoke. It was one thing to talk to yourself on a bus, another in a neighborhood like this one. "If only they could see Elwood—now *that* would clutch their pearls."

Elwood put his paws to his cheek in feigned shock.

"We shouldn't be here," Uncle said, facing the bungalow. Miniature American flags lined the walkway, and on the door was a spring wreath with anemones, freesia, and a variety of vibrant ranunculus. "There's something off about all this. Why'd Mai take off like that?"

Cherry twisted her mouth. "Maybe she was scared. Maybe she went to the hospital for her leg—I don't know. I guess we'll find out."

Elwood hopped down the walkway to the porch and looked through the transom window. Cherry and the gang followed.

"I want to see!" Daisy shouted, climbing up and onto Elwood's back. "I see that man with the nose thing from the place last night."

"What man with the nose thing? Flop?" said Cherry.

"Yeah!"

"What the hell is he doing here?"

Daisy shrugged. "He's sitting on the couch reading."

"What's he reading, the novel adaptation of the movie *Singles*?" Cherry laughed at her own joke and held up her hand to Elwood for a high five. Elwood looked at Cherry, his face as inanimate as ever.

Daisy shrugged. "I don't get it."

"Let's get this over with," said Cherry, and knocked on the door.

A moment later Flop was standing before them, wearing a large, colorful striped shirt and baggy slacks. He squinted in the sunlight.

"Yeah?" he said. Then added, "Oh, hey. You're the girl from the club, right?"

"Hi," said Cherry with a quick smile. "Do you know Mai?"

"Mai? Yeah, she's my girlfriend. Why?"

"It's just that…why didn't you say you knew her last night at the Gut Punch. You acted like she was a stranger."

"I was pretty drunk. Probably didn't know who you were talking about—how did you know where I lived?"

Uncle walked into the house, looked around, and said, "It smells like soup farts in here."

"Mai isn't home right now," said Flop, "but she should be soon. You want to come in and wait? I've got beer, coffee—weed if that's your thing." He stood to the side to let Cherry in.

"Cherry," shouted Uncle. "Don't you dare—you don't know this guy from Adam. For all you know he's got lotion, a basket, and a little dog."

Cherry rolled her eyes.

Flop's face turned red. "Oh, sorry, I didn't—"

"Oh, no—that eye roll wasn't for you. I was thinking about something an uncle said to me one time, about entering a stranger's home. He's a relic, my uncle. But I suppose he's got a point. Mind if I

leave her bag? I promised I'd get it back for her—
that's what I was doing last night at the Gut Punch.
How's she doing, anyway? Better, I hope?"

"That's very considerate, Cherry," said Flop
as he accepted Mai's bag. "I'll let her know you
stopped by. And yes, she's doing a lot better. But
she'd kill me if I didn't get your address. To send a
thank you letter, you know?"

Cherry hesitated, then looked through her bag
for a pen and paper.

Daisy moved closer, waving to get Cherry's
attention.

"Not now," Cherry said under her breath.

"Excuse me?" asked Flop.

"Oh, nothing, just talking to myself. A bad
habit—but hey, I never get lonely."

Daisy spoke again, "Mama, how does he know
your name?"

How did he know her name? She never gave it,
had she?

"You know," said Cherry, "I'm sure I'll run into
Mai soon enough. I need to jet. Nice to meet you…"

"Owen."

"Nice to meet you, Owen. Have a great day."

"Wait a second," said Owen. "What's your name?"

"My name?" said Cherry glancing over at Daisy.

Owen rubbed the back of his neck and smiled.
"Yeah."

Daisy looked up at Cherry. Uncle clinched his
fists. Elwood tilted his head.

"It's Cherry…"

CHAPTER NINE

SEVEN YEARS EARLIER

"**D**ad?" said Cherry.

"Yeah, baby."

"This might be the best casserole you've ever made." Cherry leaned back on the sofa, the bowl of food on her lap.

They were watching one of her favorite flicks, *Cleopatra*, starring Elizabeth Taylor. Her dad would groan whenever she'd put it on, but after a few minutes he would be caught up in the story and forget he was sick of it.

"Was it like this when you lived in Egypt?"

"Yes. Everyone wore gold and—hey, I had a big bathtub with ladies standing around in my place just like that!"

"You're such a nerd, Dad."

"Okay, so maybe it wasn't exactly like that. But man, the people are beautiful. I'd love to go back and visit."

Her dad looked off into the distance and smiled, then shook his head. "Maybe some day."

Cherry paused, then said, "Dad?"

"Yeah?"

"What's that book in your closet?" Cherry regretted saying it as soon as it came out.

"What are you talking about? You been going through my stuff after I told you not to?" Her dad set his bowl of food on the coffee table, the fork clanging against the side of the bowl. "It's none of your business, is what it is."

"Sorry. I just—"

"What else did you see?"

"Dad, I—"

Cherry's dad got up, looked out the blinds, then sat back down. "It's an antique. Probably worth a lot of money, so let's just keep it down, okay?"

"Okay..."

"It might be worth enough to get us out of this cramped place. Maybe we'll move to the suburbs. Would you like that?"

"Sure, Dad. Sounds nice. But...where did you get it?"

"Someone gave it to me," said her dad, then looked down at his bowl. "What should we have for dessert?"

CHAPTER TEN

OASIS OR BLUR?

herry handed the application to the clerk behind the counter at the record shop. He took it without looking up and set it in a stack with a dozen other applications.

"Lot of people want this job, eh?" Cherry leaned against the counter, nearly knocking down a CD display.

"Yeah."

"When will you start interviewing?"

"Don't know."

Cherry smiled as politely as she could manage. "Oasis or Blur?"

"What?"

"What team are you on? Oasis or Blur?"

The clerk looked up. "Blur, obviously."

"Nice try," said Cherry walking over to a crate, where she began flipping through the records. "The correct answer is Pulp."

Uncle leaned against a shelf with a look of disgust on his face. "Wouldn't be my first choice, but hey, a job is a job, and money is money."

"Where would you work?" asked Cherry without looking up. "I mean, if you weren't in my head."

"Don't know. Open up a club—but not like that dive from last night. No, somethin' classy. Get an act like Louis Prima and Keely Smith. Serve Champagne in cocktail glasses...real classy."

Uncle smiled and stared out the window.

"I'm sure that would be a hit with the kids," Cherry said. "So, that dude Owen is a weirdo, right?" She smiled awkwardly as a girl walked by, then continued, "I'm so confused about what he was doing at Mai's place."

"Don't know," said Uncle. "But I had a look at his computer while you were chattin'."

"Oh yeah?"

"Yeah, he had your file up—your state assistance record."

"And you're just now telling me this?"

"You don't leave a lot of oxygen for the room, Cher."

Elwood scratched his ear.

"Why should I even believe you?" she said. "There's no way you could see something I can't. *You are me.* Anyway, we'll talk more about this at home. We should move on to the next failure."

Cherry thanked the clerk and exited the record store.

Out front, sitting on the hood of his black Chevy sedan and playing with his nose ring, was Owen. "Cherry, Cherry, quite contrary."

Daisy hid behind Cherry's legs.

"What the fuck—are you following me? If you think I'm a little lamb lost in the woods, you better think—"

"I'm just here to deliver a gift—for being a humanitarian and fetching Mai's bag. It should be the norm, right? Being a good neighbor and all that. But it's not." Owen slid off the hood of the car, walked around to the passenger side window, and pulled out a ten-inch-square painting canvas. He held it out to Cherry.

Uncle hovered between them, a rage-filled, hairless gorilla wearing a sleeveless white t-shirt. He would have been an intimidating sight if he wasn't a figment of Cherry's imagination.

Cherry thought about going back into the record shop or booking it down the street. There was something off about this guy Owen. She was sure she didn't tell him where she was headed. Reluctantly, she reached through Uncle, took the canvas from Owen's hands, and looked down at the painting: it was a detailed portrait of herself sitting on a golden throne, the colors swirling and vibrant as if they might spill right off the painting. Behind her were three silhouettes stretched against a cement wall: a rabbit-man, a square lug, and a child with pigtails.

Cherry gasped and backed away from Owen. It wasn't possible. How could he know about her Alternates?

Owen grinned and got into his car. "See ya around, Cherry."

QUEEN OF BROKEN BRAINS

CHAPTER ELEVEN

ncle was adamant that they keep to the apartment for a few days. Cherry acted annoyed, but she was creeped out by Owen showing up at the record shop and the portrait he'd given to her, so maybe it wasn't such a bad idea to stick close to home for a little while.

She looked at the portrait; it didn't make sense. The only person who knew about her Alternates was her doctor. And why was she sitting on a throne in this painting? She sure as hell didn't feel powerful.

Her Majesty, Cherry Kills—the queen of broken brains, she thought.

A steady downpour of icy rain made the seclusion less oppressive; she wouldn't go out in this if she could. Cherry curled up on the living room couch drinking a Snapple and examining the portrait, occasionally looking up to see Daisy and Elwood playing Rock, Paper, Scissors.

Uncle stood as still as a statue, watching the street below. "You never thanked us for saving your life."

"Okay, sure—thank you," said Cherry. "Now that we've gotten that out of the way, why are you still here? You don't want to be here, and I'd like to live my life. So maybe it's time you—" Cherry motioned to the door. "You know?"

Daisy came over and sat next to Cherry. "Why would we leave you? We love you."

Cherry stood and walked over to the window. It was quiet out on the street with only the occasional car splashing by.

"Maybe I don't love you," she said. "Go haunt someone else."

In that moment, Cherry hated the sound of her own voice.

Daisy lowered her head and picked at a tiny embroidered pink flower on her dress.

Uncle placed a hand on Daisy's shoulder and scowled at Cherry. "She's just havin' a moment, Dayz. She thinks we're not real, yet here we are, havin' a fight."

Cherry stuck her teeth out and wiggled her nose. "What do you think, giant rabbit-man? Are you real?"

Elwood shrugged.

"I can always rely on you for an honest reaction," said Cherry.

"Explain why we're in that painting, Cupcake," said Uncle, looking at his square nails.

"My therapist must have told somebody about you, and now they're trying to take advantage of me. It's got to—"

Uncle laughed, walked over to the couch, and sat. "Take advantage of you? You got a stash of money hidden away I ain't aware of?"

Cherry picked up a pillow, screamed into it, then calmly set the pillow next to her on the couch. "Unless you want to discuss Liz Taylor's eyebrows, we're done talking. I'm going to watch *Cleopatra* and try to finish this disgusting Snapple, and you're going to sit there quietly. Understood?" She picked up the remote and turned on the television set.

Daisy picked up a pillow and handed it to Uncle. "Your turn."

Cherry tried to focus on her movie, but her mind kept drifting back to Mai. If they were a couple and he was at the Gut Punch, why didn't she mention him to Cherry? Either she was withholding this information or Owen had lied. The latter seemed likely.

She thought back to her first interaction with Mai over two months ago when she had approached Cherry's table holding a novel. "I realized this morning I have two copies of this book," she'd said, "and I saw you sitting here alone with nothing to distract you from this place's decor. Having a good read might help with that."

Cherry hadn't told Mai she was surrounded by three big distractions at that very moment, she looked over the top of Mai's novel and said, "What is it?"

Mai told her it was *Diary of a Madman*.

"I've got my own diary, thanks," she'd said, but there was something familiar in Mai's face that softened Cherry's response, and she'd accepted the book, although she never actually opened it.

Cherry turned off the television, walked to

the bookshelf, and pulled out the book Mai had given her. She considered reading it, thumbed through a few pages, but seeing a passage about talking dogs, felt it was a little too close to home. She was just about to place it back on the shelf, when something on the back page caught her eye. It was a sketch of a woman who looked a lot like Cherry's mom. But that wasn't possible. Still, she couldn't take her eyes off of the sketch, and she couldn't help the overwhelming feeling that this was no coincidence.

EIGHTY-SIXED

CHAPTER TWELVE

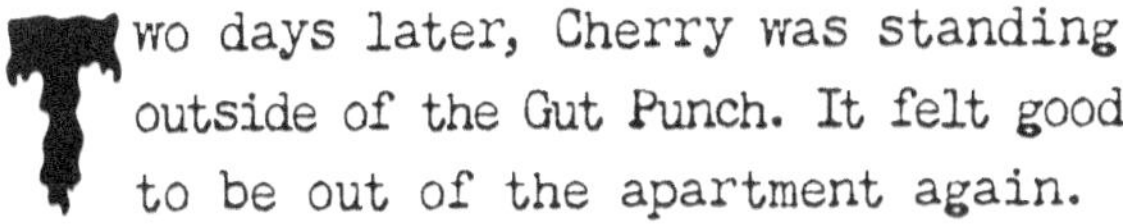

wo days later, Cherry was standing outside of the Gut Punch. It felt good to be out of the apartment again.

"Wait here," Uncle said, strolling into the club. He was against coming back to the Gut Punch, thought it was reckless and unnecessary—which, maybe it was—but Cherry told him he had no choice in the matter. Still, she didn't want him complaining the entire time, so she told him he could go to the backroom and scope it out first.

The doorman shook his head as Cherry approached. "I don't think so, honey. You're eighty-sixed."

"Eighty-sixed? For what?"

"I think you know why." The doorman got up from his stool and blocked the door.

"Was it because I called you sweet as pie? I apologize. You're as bitter as an orange rind. Better?"

"Who do you think had to clean that back room up at the end of the night? Who do you think they get to do that bullshit?"

Cherry made a pouty face. "Sucks to be you, champ. Hey, can I ask you a question?"

"Will you leave after?"

Cherry always seemed to have a way with getting what she wanted. Ramon said it was the gift of gab, but it always felt like something more than just being able to bullshit.

"Deal," she said.

"Ask away."

"Last night, that chick who was painting your mural…was she with anyone?" Cherry leaned against the brick wall. Inside the club Uncle was returning from the back, looking around with his chest puffed out.

"Yeah, she was with some dude. He got pretty hammered during the headliner. He started talking all this crazy shit to anyone and everyone—dude tried to punch me! I ended up clocking homie in the jaw. You know him?"

"Dude's a creeper," she said. "I think he's stalking me or something…I don't know."

"Yeah, fuck that guy. Steer clear of him. He was talking real crazy—said he was going to be my king one day or something. He said that right before I laid him out. When he came to, he mumbled some shit about a Dog Star, got up, and stumbled on down the road."

Cherry narrowed her eyes. "Dog Star? Weird. My dad called me that sometimes." She thought back to when she was a girl; her dad told her about the night he'd first kissed her mom, beneath the velvety Egyptian sky. He said she pointed up to the brightest star in the sky and told him about the Dog Star. And that when Cherry was born, it was almost like that star had come straight down to Earth.

Uncle came out, turned the corner, and started back down the street toward the apartment. "Mark ain't glowin', and someone threw paint over the mural."

"You okay?" said the doorman. "You having an aneurysm or something?"

"Sorry—I'm good," said Cherry. "What's up with that mural in there? That chick come back and paint the rest yet?"

"That's another reason I punched that clown last night. He threw paint all over the mural. I was here all night cleaning up after that fool." The doorman shook his head.

Cherry looked to the back of the club—how did Uncle see that the mural had been painted over? She leaned in and whispered to the bouncer, "And nothing weird happened back there while you were cleaning up?"

"He didn't come back, if that's what you mean."

Cherry paused, then said, "Yes, that's exactly what I mean. Well, I appreciate you, champ. Real heroes don't wear capes and all that shit. Stay safe."

"You too. But really, don't come back."

"You love me, don't pretend otherwise."

Cherry followed behind Uncle and her Alternates. She looked up to the sky, but there were no stars, only dark clouds. And there were no answers, only more questions.

CHAPTER THIRTEEN

KILL YOUR TELEVISION

Up ahead of Cherry, walking down the stained but vacuumed floral carpet leading to her apartment, Daisy stretched her arms and yawned. Elwood patted her head, and then looked back at Cherry with that expressionless face of his. It was a face that should have creeped her out: cold, almost like a Halloween mask permanently affixed to his head, but it was oddly comforting to her. It reminded her of a stuffed animal that she had when she was just a girl. A gift from her mom before she left, her dad had said.

"Well, is that it?" asked Uncle. "Can we get back to looking for a job?"

Cherry shrugged. "Who the hell would hire me? I wouldn't hire me."

"You can work at Black Garlic. Ramon loves you, and he's a *compare*." Uncle nodded as though the matter was settled. Then he looked up, watching a moth caught in the tulip-shaped sconce flutter about, casting shadows on the wall.

"Yeah, maybe…" Cherry went to insert her key in the door, but when she touched the doorknob, the door opened on its own. She raised a brow. *Cleopatra* was soundlessly playing on the television. "Did I leave the TV on?"

Uncle turned around as Cherry was heading inside. "Cherry, wait!"

The door slammed shut behind her. She turned around and pulled on the door, but it wouldn't budge. Uncle slammed into the door repeatedly, the door shaking with each attempt.

How did it shake? He's not real.

Cherry looked around the room. On the wall above the television was the same symbol from the club, glowing. Pulsing. Threatening.

"Eff..." Cherry put up her fists.

"Cherry," shouted Uncle from the other side of the door. "What's going on in there? You okay?"

"There's a glowing symbol on the wall," she replied, "but I'm not underwater, so...okay-ish?"

The movie cut to static, the snow lighting up the room with noisy whites.

"Well, now I'm a little freaked out," she said. "We've got a 'they're here' moment happening. Could really use some help."

At first it was only a finger, too thin to be an adult's, too long to be a child's. Then came the hand; blue veins like worms pulsed under translucent skin. Its arthritic knuckles grabbed at the air. The knobby shillelagh-arm flung about, protruding from the television screen.

Cherry tried the door again, but it wouldn't budge.

A second arm came through the screen. Then a third, fourth, fifth and sixth arm—until there were too many to count, all grabbing toward

Cherry, who circled away from the television into the kitchen, pulled a knife from the knife block, and gritted her teeth. She never thought she'd be so desperate to have Uncle and her Alternates at her side, but she was alone in this fight.

She ran back to the door and tried again, but it still wouldn't budge.

Then, all of the arms retreated back into the television. Cherry exhaled.

A body exploded from the television in a wave of bubblegum-pink afterbirth, splattering across the walls and onto Cherry's face and neck.

"Uncle, I need you!"

The creature got to its feet, dragging itself up off the floor using the back of the couch, trying to find its balance like a wobbly-legged nightmare colt. It was slim-faced and wore a long woeful expression, and its large, oval eyes were filled with the same noisy static as the television. It licked its lips with a pale-pink tongue and sniffed at the air.

Cherry ran for the bedroom as the creature found its legs, darting to cut her off, sliding and crashing into her bookshelf. It opened its mouth and a deafening static filled the room. Cherry covered her ears and stumbled backwards. This was the end. But hey, at least she wouldn't have to look for a job now.

Two more of the same nightmare creatures climbed out of the television. One of the monsters was missing its legs, the other was only a body with a gnarled arm sticking out from where its head should have been, dragging itself across the floor, leaving a trail of pink goo.

SMASH!

The door exploded open as Uncle came flying into the room, raining down splintered wood and metal hinges. Elwood and Daisy followed.

Cherry's lip quivered. Maybe it wasn't so bad to have Alternates, if only so she wouldn't die alone. *But how did Uncle break down the door?* she thought. She wondered if this was it, and if she was in the midst of a full-on psychotic break. But there was no time to consider it—break or not, this was happening.

"Mama, what are these things?" Daisy shouted.

"Maybe I've been watching too much TV!"

Uncle kicked the legless creature's head like a football, killing it instantly, but the creature with an arm for a head grabbed his leg, sinking its slender fingers into Uncle's flesh as more of them began to climb out of the television set.

Cherry yelled, "Daisy, unplug the set!"

Daisy ran over and unplugged the television set, but it still glowed, and the creatures kept coming. Elwood hopped to the back of the set and kicked it onto its face. Then he sat on it, folded his arms, and did a quick head nod to say, "And that's that."

A static-eyed nightmare skulked, dragging its long fingers along the side of the wall, leaving four delicate black lines, as if each fingertip were a soldering iron. Crimson drool extended from its lips.

Cherry held her knife out in front of her. "I'll mess you up, my dude. Back off!"

Uncle threw the arm-headed nightmare out of the apartment, and when it crossed the threshold it sizzled, then vanished.

Daisy shouted, "Did you see that? The monsters can't get us if we're not in the apartment!"

"She's right!" shouted Uncle. "Cherry! Run!"

Cherry pivoted to run, but a slender hand shot out and grabbed her wrist. The pain was intense; her flesh hissed and smoked. She thought it fitting that she should feel the same pain as her dad when he died. To be burned alive felt right.

She looked into the television-eyes of the creature and remembered a time when she was twelve; she and her dad were already living at the Sequoia apartments. He'd passed out drunk on the couch again, this time while smoking. She'd come out of her room because the static from the television had woken her from sleep, and the couch was ablaze. She'd thrown a pot of water onto the couch to put it out, but it went all over the television too. The TV set was ruined, of course.

Cherry grabbed the disgusting Snapple sitting on the counter and threw it into the noisy eyes of the creature.

It opened its mouth and hissed, but it let go of Cherry's arm. Then she ran to the door and out into the hallway. Her Alternates followed.

The creature slid to the door, but it didn't come out into the hallway. It turned its head to the left, then the right, hissed once more for good measure, then plodded off to the back of the room where it crouched in the darkness, its eyes glowing with static for a moment before *Cleopatra* came on. Two tiny Elizabeth Taylors sat on a throne in the creature's eyes.

"Didn't I tell you that flavor was disgusting?" Cherry said.

Her Alternates didn't laugh. Cherry didn't either. She dropped the knife and cried.

CHAPTER FOURTEEN

CHERRY, CHERRY, QUITE CONTRARY

own on the street, Cherry looked up at her darkened apartment window and blew on her wrist. Her arm throbbed where the static-eyed creature had grabbed her with its molten grip, but the cool air helped.

"That was fun," she said, then turned and walked down the street. Where she was going, she wasn't sure. Anywhere far away from what had just happened would do.

"This ain't going away on its own," said Uncle, following behind Cherry. "It's that floppy-haired doofus. It has to be! Those doodles or somethin'? A hex?"

Elwood nodded in agreement while Daisy, jumping and splashing in a puddle in the middle of the street, smiled as if nothing had happened.

"This might shock you, big guy," Cherry said to Uncle, "but I agree. That floppy-haired creeper made this happen."

"We gotta call the cops and—"

Cherry turned to face Uncle. "Officer, a monster came out of my TV."

"You have to tell someone about—"

"Officer, I was attacked by a nightclub squid— oh, but don't worry, my imaginary friend saved my life."

Daisy laughed and walked side by side with Cherry. "You're funny, Mama."

Cherry pulled away from Daisy and stormed down the street. "Ugh, shut the fuck up, Daisy—can't you see I'm not in the mood. I'm not your goddamn mama. I can't even take care of myself." Cherry regretted saying it as soon as it came out of her mouth, but it was true—she wasn't her mama. Daisy wasn't even real. A made-up little girl to cope with the horrors of this world. Why a little girl? She couldn't say.

Daisy lowered her head.

Elwood knelt and wiped the tears from Daisy's eyes.

Cherry walked on. It was either a motel or Ramon's, and seeing how she didn't have any money, Black Garlic it was. Besides, she needed a friendly face right now. A real one.

* * *

It was well past closing time at Black Garlic, but Ramon was still inside the dining room folding napkins. Cherry tapped on the window and waved. She explained to Ramon the situation; a man was stalking her, and she didn't feel safe—all true, of course—but she left out the part about the mural coming to life, the static-eyed creatures in her apartment, and—even though she liked Ramon more than most people—she continued to keep her Alternates a secret.

Cherry covered up her wrist with her left hand; it throbbed where the static-eyed creature had grabbed her.

Ramon ushered her inside the restaurant.

"I'm not sure why I'm here…I should go."

"A stiff drink first, then decide what you want to do." He led her to a small room in the back with a couch, a desk, and a computer. He picked up a bottle of whiskey from the desk and poured the brown liquid into two glasses. "Bottoms up."

Cherry raised her glass. "May the Devil learn we're in Hell half an hour before he's ready for us."

Ramon laughed and shook his head. "You know, if you want to sleep here tonight you're more than welcome. Solid locks on this place. Security system. I have a blanket in my car, should I go grab it?"

Cherry looked at the couch—she was exhausted. "You sure you don't mind?"

"I insist. Just for the night! No dogs or cats, right?"

"What about rabbits?"

Ramon chuckled and went to fetch the blanket from his car.

Cherry walked around the office. On the wall, an award given by the mayor for Best New Restaurant. Next to that, a framed newspaper clipping declaring Black Garlic as "The hottest restaurant in the City." Cherry loved the food at Black Garlic, but it certainly wasn't the hottest restaurant. Even on the weekends it wasn't busy, not by hottest restaurant standards.

"Not sure how we're all gonna fit," said Uncle,

pointing to the couch where Elwood and Daisy were cuddling.

"We? You three are waiting in the dining room while I sleep—"

Ramon walked into the room. "You say something?"

Cherry stepped away from the desk and smiled. "Bad habit—I talk to myself when I'm stressed, ya know?"

"Well, tell yourself not to set off the alarm tonight, okay? Just stay put, and if you need anything, here's my number. Call me, no matter how late. I should get going before I fall asleep on my feet. You all good?"

"All good, Ramon. And thank you. You're a lifesaver. I'll make it up to you. I swear."

"Yeah, yeah. Go get some sleep."

After Ramon had locked the door, Cherry motioned to Daisy and Elwood to get up, stretched out on the couch, and stared at the ceiling. *I've been watching too much television anyway*, she thought.

Elwood went to explore the dining room.

"Let me guess," said Uncle. "We're going to see Bullring tomorrow?"

"What else is there to do?" said Cherry. "We need to find out what the hell is going on. Besides, he owes me money for trashing my apartment— that's going to come out of my deposit."

Cherry turned to face Uncle. "I can't help thinking this is somehow connected to that symbol I see in my dreams." Cherry narrowed her eyes. "And the book my dad kept hidden in his closet, before it burned up in the fire. You know, those marks on the wall are Egyptian—I'm sure of it. But what does Owen have to do with any of that? And how the hell does he know about you three? None of this makes sense."

Elwood rushed into the office, motioning to come quickly.

Cherry, Uncle, and Daisy followed Elwood to the dining room and looked out the front window. Written across the front window in black, dripping like wet eyeliner, were the words:

CHERRY, CHERRY, QUITE CONTRARY.

Cherry shook her head and backed away. "He's been following us."

EIGHT YEARS EARLIER

"This way!" Cherry pulled her dad's arm and stomped toward the case displaying the Vulture Crown of Isis. She felt light and happy. Just like she did every Saturday during their excursions to the museum.

Her dad shook his head. "Mosey, Cher. We're moseying."

"Do you think it was really Isis's?"

"You think Isis would let a museum have her crown?"

"It's still cool. When I'm old and rich I'm going to have a crown just like this. I'll wear it wherever I go. Grocery shopping, dentist—"

"You'd wear this thing to the dentist?" Her dad laughed.

"Everywhere."

"You're so much like your mom—it's scary," her dad joked, but Cherry could hear the sadness behind his laughter.

Cherry walked to the next exhibit. A sandstone cat looked back at her from wide curious eyes.

"Do you ever miss her?"

Her dad paused, then said, "Yes and no."

Cherry thought it best to let it go, but then he continued.

"For a long time I was angry at her for leaving— wished I'd never met her. But not anymore. I look at you and...I wouldn't want to live in this world without you, Dogstar. You're everything to me. Do I think about her? All the time. Do I wish she'd come back? No—no I don't. That page has been turned, you know? But there's something I'm sure about: wherever she is, she's thinking of you. She loved you, Cherry. She knew you'd be okay—you've got that huge hummingbird heart."

* * *   EIGHT YEARS EARLIER   * * *

CHAPTER SIXTEEN

KEEP IT A SECRET

"**D**ad," said Cherry. "Why do you have a gun?" Her dad's face morphed like it always did in these dreams.

"To provide." His voice boomed and echoed off the eggshell walls, threatening to crack them open and spill whatever dreams are made from all over the pea-green shag.

Cherry felt small. "I don't need anything but you," she said.

Her dad smiled. "I'm dead." Then the symbol, with its golden flourishes and falcon and its ever-watching eye, beamed from the center of his forehead like a floodlight, scorching Cherry's retinas.

"Eset," her dad's voice boomed. "Keep it secret."

Cherry woke to the sound of Ramon's keys jingling in the front door of the restaurant. *Eset.* Her mom's name. But what did her mom have to do with the fire?

Just a dream.

"Cherry!" he shouted. "You okay?"

Cherry stepped over a sleeping Daisy and Elwood, who were curled up together on the floor. Uncle was sitting in the dining room, looking out the window. He'd been there all night. Keeping watch.

"Jesus, you weren't kidding about this guy." Ramon motioned to the window. "What a creep. Do you want me to call the police for you?"

Cherry shook her head. "I'll pay for that. I'm sorry—"

"Nonsense—nothing to be sorry about. I'll have that cleaned off in no time." Ramon looked around the room. "Well, what do you say I make some coffee?" Ramon headed toward the kitchen.

"Thank you, Ramon. You're a dream come true."

Daisy came out and sat next to Uncle. Neither of them said a word.

Cherry whispered, "I had another one of those nightmares."

Uncle and Daisy continued to look out the window at the street.

"What's this, the silent treatment? Fine by me. Finally, some peace and quiet. Anyway, after I get my caffeine, we're going to confront this bozo. I can't live like this." Cherry looked at the graffiti in silence, feeling more alone than she'd ever felt in her life.

Ramon came from the kitchen with coffee in hand. "Coffee for my friend Cherry."

* * * KEEP IT A SECRET * * *

SORRY, BABE.

CHAPTER SEVENTEEN

wen's car wasn't on the street or in the driveway at 6666 Cedar. The tortoiseshell cat cleaned her bib, unaware of or unimpressed by Uncle, who tramped through the flowerbeds looking into the windows to make sure the coast was clear. He eventually waved Cherry, Elwood, and Daisy over.

"Must be out drawing his doodles," said Uncle. "Where to now?"

Cherry walked toward the rear of the house.

"Hold up," said Uncle, trundling after her. "What's the plan, Cupcake?"

Cherry shrugged. "We're just having a look."

Daisy sat down in the driveway and pushed at a pillbug with her dainty finger while Elwood lounged on the grass sniffing at a violet he plucked from a flowerbed.

"You were rough on her, Cher," Uncle said, and nodded toward Daisy.

Cherry climbed the steps to the porch and looked through the window. The kitchen was vacant. "Daisy will be alright—she's not even real. She's me. Or I'm her—something like that."

"Whatever you think we are, would it kill you to show us a little respect?"

Cherry rolled her eyes, then tried the door: it was unlocked. "Elwood, you and Daisy keep watch. Uncle, you're with me."

The house was neat, organized, and without a speck of dust. The only sign anyone had been living there at all was a notepad and pencil on the coffee table in the living room.

Cherry read the top page of the notepad aloud, "'She's at Black Garlic.' Well, I guess there's no doubt about it now. He's our guy. Let's get the hell out of here before—"

A muffled shout resonated from somewhere in the house.

Uncle clenched his fists. "Is it doofus?"

"No," Cherry replied. "Sounded like a chick—"

Another shout, this time clearer. "Someone, help me!"

Cherry headed for a door off the hallway.

Uncle moved in front of her. "Cherry, this don't feel right. We need to go. Now."

Out front, Daisy and Elwood sat on the stoop, keeping watch. Cherry could see the tops of Elwood's fuzzy ears. She moved around Uncle and opened the door, then stared down into the basement. It was dark.

"Hello," cried the voice. "Who's there? Please help me—"

Cherry shouted back, "Are you okay?"

"Oh, thank God—please get me out of here before he comes back!"

Cherry clicked on the light and descended the stairs. Uncle followed, grumbling his disapproval.

At the bottom of the steps, Cherry gasped.

The room was full of artifacts; stone ankhs hung

on the walls, canopic jars crowded the room, and sleek, granite sphinx cats lounged in the corners. And there amongst these cultural treasures was the cotton-candy-haired girl, bound and blindfolded on a golden throne.

It was Mai.

"This don't feel right, Cher," said Uncle, looking around the room. "We gotta go."

Cherry stepped backward up the steps.

"Please, no—don't go! My name is Mai Ito. Please you have to help me. I—"

Ito, that last name sounded familiar to Cherry, but she couldn't place where she'd heard it before. She looked at Uncle and shrugged. She couldn't just leave Mai here. She wouldn't leave anyone behind—never again. She removed Mai's blindfold. "Everything is going to be alright. It's me, Cherry. From Black Garlic. We're going to get you out of here."

"Thank God! How did you know I was here?" Mai asked, her eyes adjusting to the light.

"I didn't!" Cherry pulled the knot from the ropes around Mai's wrists. "This creep Owen has been stalking me. He said you were his girlfriend?"

Mai rubbed her wrists and stood. "Hell no— he's insane. We used to work at a museum in San Jose together, you know, selling keychains and sweaters at the gift shop. He has always been a bit off, but nothing like this."

Uncle stood at the foot of the stairs, listening for Daisy.

Cherry got to work untethering Mai's legs. The rope was thick, but not tied particularly tight, almost like Owen had considered Mai's comfort. "What does he want with us? And how the hell is he—"

"He said something about an antique book," interrupted Mai.

The book, thought Cherry. "What does a book have to do with me?"

"I don't know…he said you have a picture or something? Maybe a photograph? Said if I didn't help him lure you to the Gut Punch, that night you found me crying at the restaurant, he'd kill me. He's nuts—he would have done it. I'm so sorry." Mai wept.

It was all so hazy, the night her dad had died in the fire, but she remembered the photograph falling out of the book all those years ago. And she remembered him holding it out to her, just before the fire took him. It was hard to remember anything else. She had blacked out, and when she came to, Elwood was there, carrying her through the smoke and flames to safety.

"I don't have anything," said Cherry. "Whatever he's looking for…everything burned up in a fire years ago."

"He said something about a symbol," replied Mai. "A hieroglyphic." Mai stood and wiped her eyes.

"I don't have anything from that night—nothing besides heavy baggage and zero desire to attend a barbecue." Cherry started toward the stairs.

Mai pulled out a Sharpie. "Did it look like this?" The symbol she drew on the wall looked similar in style to the one from Cherry's dream, as well as the one from the Gut Punch and her apartment, but it wasn't the same. The symbol in her dream had something that made her feel…electric.

"Not exactly," said Cherry, then turned to go up the stairs. "We should get out—"

"Sorry, babe," said Mai.

Cherry whipped around just in time to see and feel a heavy object crack against her head. She crumpled.

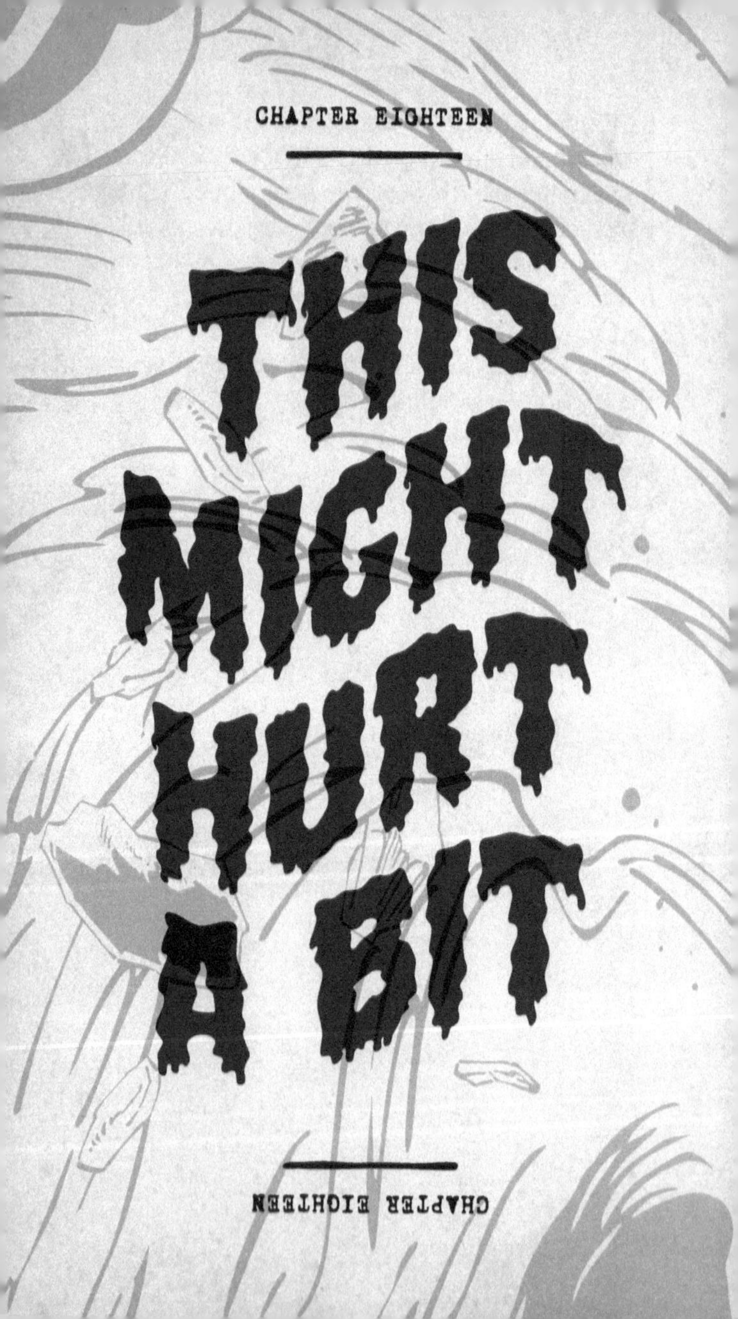
CHAPTER EIGHTEEN

THIS MIGHT HURT A BIT

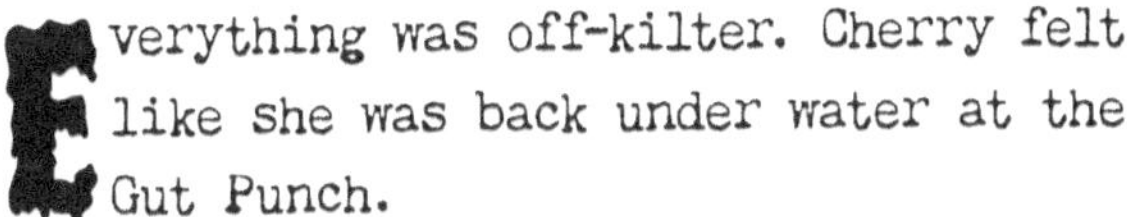verything was off-kilter. Cherry felt like she was back under water at the Gut Punch.

"Cherry!" A muffled shout. "Cherry, are you okay?" It was Uncle, but he sounded so far away. Cherry wanted to swim to him, to tell him she was fine. Just a little wobbly. Just a little…mixed up. Then, there was Mai's boot, pushing her.

"Babe? You okay, babe? I hit you harder than I meant to. Don't you go dying on me, Cherry. I need you." Mai pulled Cherry up to the throne and tied her wrists to the chair's arms.

Cherry was still underwater, but it was shallow now. She felt herself floating to the surface and then, when she'd finally shaken off the blow, the pain set in.

"The fuck…"

"The fuck is right," said Mai. "I need to lay off the Frappuccinos. That was pure caffeine strength right there. Unintentional, Cherry my dear—only meant to stun you!"

Uncle was as close as he could get to Mai, seething. He looked like an enraged gorilla. "I'll kill her, Cherry. I'll rip her goddamn head off—"

"Settle down," said Cherry.

"Who?" replied Mai. "Me? Or are you talking about the big dude breathing down my neck?"

Uncle stepped back in shock.

Cherry shook her head. "How…"

Mai smiled, then walked over to where she'd

drawn the mark on the wall with her Sharpie. She took out her pen and drew a new symbol directly beneath the first. It was like the glyphs on the walls at the Gut Punch and her apartment, only this mark was larger, with three squares layered one on top of the other. For some reason, it reminded Cherry of Uncle. Then Mai took her pen and drew a line down the center.

Uncle looked at Cherry, concern in his eyes, then vanished.

Cherry felt like she'd been hit a second time; Uncle was gone. Cherry shouted, "What did you do?"

Mai shrugged. "I have a little confession. I haven't been completely honest with you."

"No shit." Cherry rolled her wrists beneath the rope, but it was no use, she couldn't break free. "Listen, you clearly want something from me, but you should know I don't have much. Unless you want a television set?"

"Cherry, your dad killed my dad." Mai sniffed the tip of her Sharpie. "Thoughts?"

Cherry stared at Mai in disbelief.

Mai added, "God, I love the smell of ink. It's like smelling possibilities—anything you can think of, you can create it. Or you can destroy with it, if that's your thing. For me, it depends on my mood." Mai drew another glyph on the wall that looked similar to the one she'd drawn when Uncle disappeared, but instead of the squares, this one had two loops that looked like ears sticking up from the top of it. Mai drew a line down the center.

Upstairs, Daisy screamed and then shouted, "Mama! Elwood! He's gone!"

Cherry struggled to free herself. She had to stop this. Sure, she didn't want her Alternates around all the time, but she'd gotten used to having them in her life, and if they were somehow real....

"What do you mean my dad killed your dad?" said Cherry.

"Your dad murdered my dad. Well, that's not entirely true—one of his buddies killed my dad. But your dad was with them, and by all accounts, he was the one who set the whole thing up."

Cherry shook her head. "You're crazy—why would he have done that?"

Mai leaned against the basement wall. "Why does anyone do anything? Money, honey! Dad was a well-known and respected supplier of artifacts for some of the top museums around the world. But he also supplied artifacts for private collectors, and that wasn't exactly on the up and up. If you know what I mean."

"He was a crook?" said Cherry.

"When Dad was murdered, I inherited all of this—" Mai waved her hands around at the artifacts surrounding them in the basement. "Sell all this shit and you're looking at a pretty comfy life. Your dad knew about all this—I suppose he felt like he was owed a slice of the pie, not just a few crumbs."

Cherry looked around the room for some way to

get out of the mess she was in.

Mai continued, "I didn't just meet your dad the night of the robbery, he'd been to the house a hundred times before."

Cherry looked up at Mai.

Mai raised her eyebrows and smiled at Cherry. "Your dad was a big dude. I believe in the thieving world he'd have been called the muscle of the operation, right? My guess is that's why dad hired him, you know, to intimidate private collectors, deliver cash to and pick up artifacts from collectors who were willing. Stealing. All that sketchy shit."

Cherry wasn't naive; she'd known about her dad's unorthodox career ever since she was a girl. Even before she found his gun in the closet. The police showed up to the apartment on more than one occasion, but they never had enough to lock him up. He claimed his reasons for breaking the law were just; he needed to support his girl, and the universe was trying to keep him down. It was a sentiment Cherry had accepted when she was younger, but now that she was in the thick of life, it seemed a weak excuse.

Mai continued, "The night Dad was murdered, your dad came and forced his way into our home with four other men, shouting that they were going to blow our heads off. Do you know what that's like for a child? It's fucked, Cherry. Absolutely fucked. I was at the back of the house when your dad found me hiding beneath a table. But, you know what? He was nice to me." Mai looked at the tip of her pen, smiling. "He said he wasn't going to let anyone hurt me, and he kept his word. He didn't let any of his buddies near me. He made me feel…like a friend. Asking me how old I was—he told me he had a daughter just about my age. Said I reminded him of her. I can see it—can you?"

Cherry didn't speak.

Mai shrugged. "But then he walked around the room and took whatever he thought looked like it was worth something. Very confusing to a child desperate for protection and love. Was that the type of man he was, Cherry?"

Cherry's eyes filled with tears, but not for Mai or her own dad, but for herself; her dad had done this same thing to her more times than she could remember. He would make her feel safe and special only to make his selfish deeds seem casual and harmless.

But they did cause harm.

Mai continued, "Then I had an epiphany—I saw an opportunity to get my dad back. See, like your dad, my dad was never what some might call a 'good guy,' but we loved each other. Sure, we had our fights—I was a preteen! But we still hugged goodbye in the morning when I went off to school. We still ate dinner and watched movies together. You wouldn't have guessed it, but he was a huge fan of Steve Martin." Mai walked over to where Cherry sat on the throne.

"Listen, Mai, I'm sorry your dad—"

"Hush now, it's time to listen, not speak. In the

months leading up to the robbery, something changed in my dad, and it all started when I found a book hidden beneath the floorboards in the den."

This is all about the book, Cherry thought.

"There was a gun in there, too," said Mai, "but we'll get to that. The book was old—really old. When I opened it, a picture fell out from between its pages. A photo of my mom at a party. She was beautiful, Cherry. She was breathtaking. She'd already exited the scene when I was a baby, so I never got the chance to meet her, but this book made me feel...close to her, you know? On the back of the photo was a symbol, but when I close my eyes...I just can't seem to picture it in my mind. It's like I never saw it! I must have looked at that photo and glyph over a hundred times. But...I still can't picture it." Mai threw her hands in the air. "Isn't that something?"

Cherry thought back to the night of the fire. That was it. That's where she first saw the symbol. It was on the back of the photograph in the book. The night of the fire. But it wasn't Mai's mom in that photo. It was her mom. It was Eset.

Mai stared off into the distance, muttered something under her breath, then continued, "As I turned the pages of the book, taking in all of the hieroglyphs and unfamiliar letters, I said to myself, 'I wish I knew what this said.' And just like that, I could read the book as if it were written in English. I could interpret every hieroglyph within the book. It all made sense to me. Still, I couldn't figure out the glyph on the back of the photograph—it was almost as if the symbol was hiding its meaning from me. But the book...boy oh boy what an interesting read that was.

"When my dad got home, I told him all about it. Sure, he was angry at first, but when I began to read to him from the book...well, you can imagine his shock. I told him how powerful the book was. I told him he didn't need to work anymore—I could will money into existence. I showed him. Then, to my surprise, he told me it was my mom's book. I asked him why he'd never shown me it and do you know what he said?"

Cherry stayed silent.

"He said he'd taken it from her the night she said she was leaving, but he'd never been able to do anything with it. It didn't listen to him."

Cherry thought about how a magic book that granted wishes would be pretty damn handy right now. But more than escape, she wanted Uncle and Elwood back. She wanted to keep Daisy safe.

Mai continued, "Dad became obsessed with the book. He'd wake me in the middle of the night with a list of things for me to conjure. Sometimes, it was money. Sometimes, it was other things. I remember this one time...he asked me to make someone disappear. The man had something on my dad, and it was putting his business in jeopardy. I didn't do it—not at first. But Dad could be cold when he didn't get his way...silence can be violence, ya know? So, I did it. It didn't feel great, but sometimes we need to do things that don't feel great in order to survive."

Cherry shook her head. "Your dad should never have asked you to do such a thing, Mai. That wasn't fair."

"Life isn't fair, Cher Bear," Mai said with a thin smile. "I began to hate that book. And I began to resent my mom even more for going off to wherever the fuck she went to and leaving it with us. I even thought about burning it. So when your dad and his friends came to pick the house clean, I figured this was a chance to get it out of our lives for good. I pointed to the floorboards and told your dad how valuable the book was—that it wasn't just worth a lot of money, it could also change reality. He laughed, but when he lifted it from the hidden compartment, he gasped. Your dad didn't know what he was holding, but he knew enough about artifacts from working for my dad to understand how much money he could get for that book. Then we heard the sirens.

"I told him to take the book and leave. Dad had a hidden back exit put in when he built the place. He figured a panic room was nice, but the ability to get the hell out of the house was even better should he need to, and in his line of work…well, I suppose you know a little about that, eh? But then…then my dad saw your dad with the book in his hands, and he freaked out—his cash cow was being milked. He shouted your dad's name, and ran at him." Mai paused. "That's when one of your dad's cowardly friends shot him in the back."

Cherry sat up. "So my dad didn't kill him. Why don't you go after that dude?"

Mai smirked. "That dude is dead, Cher Bear. But it wasn't as satisfying as I'd hoped it would be, because the more I thought about it, the more I realized who the real monster was—it was your dad."

"Why? Because he stole this stupid book?"

"I pleaded with him to hand me the book—I needed to save my dad. But he wouldn't. He only wanted to get out of there. I told him to hand me the book for just one moment—just one fucking moment! So that I could say the words. So I could say, 'Daddy lives.' The cops were out front shouting to stand down, and your dad's friends were starting to panic—it was all coming to a head."

Mai walked over to the wall where she'd drawn the mark that smudged out Uncle and Elwood, and put her forehead on the stone. "I begged him, Cherry. I begged him to save my dad."

This was insane. A book that granted wishes? Cherry shook her head. "What do you want from me, Mai? My dad's been dead for seven years— seven years! And if it's some stupid book you're after—"

"Stupid book? Babe, that book is everything."

"Well, I don't have it. It probably burned up in the fire."

Mai walked over and petted Cherry's head. "I know you don't have the book, because I have it. I took it from your dad the night I shot him."

Cherry looked up at Mai. It wasn't possible.

"I didn't enjoy killing him, but it felt important to do—I knew what a selfish person could do with that book, Cherry. You understand?"

"You're telling me that you burned my dad alive when you were what? Twelve?"

"Thirteen when I finally tracked him down. It wasn't difficult—his crew weren't exactly loyal, and I had money to buy information—pillowcases full of the stuff. But I didn't burn him alive. I shot him dead."

Cherry lunged at Mai, but the ropes held fast. "He wasn't dead when you set that fire!"

Mai narrowed her eyes. For a moment, she almost looked sorry for what she'd done. Then she smirked. "So you got to say your goodbyes? That's what I was hoping for. And now I'm even more sure you have what I'm after."

Cherry gritted her teeth. "You have the book, so what the fuck are we doing here? Why now?"

"Cut the bullshit, Cher Bear. I need the photograph that was in the book. I need the symbol that was on the back. I'm not able to do what I need to without it. The book is like…well, it's like a set of keys. With the right key, and the right lock—the right glyph—I can open up doors that separate this world from another. You know, the door between what's real and what's not. But

I don't want to just open doors, Cherry, I want to be able to create things from nothing. I want to control reality, but…but most of all, I want to heal old wounds. The mark written on the photograph will allow me to do all that and so much more."

Cherry narrowed her eyes. "So what, you going to have a séance or something? Because if you want to get all witchy, knock yourself out—"

"I'm going to bring him home, Cherry." Mai smiled softly.

"Cherry, he's coming!" Daisy called out from upstairs.

Mai giggled. "She's cute. There's no denying it. But why did you conjure a little girl?"

Cherry didn't know how to respond—she didn't "conjure" anyone. "I don't get it—why the squid? Why that shit back at the apartment with those… those creatures?"

"We were testing you." Mai smiled. "We needed to find out if you knew what you were holding onto. It doesn't seem like you have much power over it. It could be you just don't have a good heart like I do."

Daisy called out again, "What should I do?"

Owen sauntered down the steps, smiling at Cherry. "Sorry about all this, Cherry, Cherry quite contrary." He patted the ancient leather-bound book in his hands. "But what can you do? Mai has something she needs to do, and I've got plans of my own. But I've asked her not to harm you, Cherry. I think you and I can be friends after all this is done."

Mai smirked. "You were hard to track down, Cherry. Owen has been a big help in getting the information I needed. Cherry the foster kid. Cherry with the stipend. Cherry with the PTSD. In return, I've promised to give him whatever he desires."

"So let's go! Did you get what you needed?" asked Owen.

In some ways, it was a relief to Cherry to see the book wasn't burned up in the fire that took her dad's life. Besides herself, it was the only thing salvaged from that night.

"Haven't asked yet." Mai smelled the pen tip again, then put a new glyph on the wall, this with two short lines coming off of the side that looked like pigtails. "You'll finally have a little peace, babe." Mai drew a line down the middle.

Cherry shouted, "No, please! Don't!" But it was too late. Daisy was gone.

"What are you waiting for?" said Owen. "Let's get this over with."

"Talk to me like that one more time..." Mai walked over and grabbed Owen by the nose ring.

"What the fuck, chill! Chill!" Owen held his hands up in surrender.

Mai let go, walked to the throne, and bent over to be face to face with Cherry. "You're going to give me the photograph—the one you say you don't have—and in return, I won't smudge out your pal Ramon."

"The photograph burned up in the fire!"

"What about the glyph—can you remember it? Enough to draw it?"

"Yes. And you could have just asked for it. What do I care about a stupid symbol?"

Mai turned to Owen. "See? See you dumb fuck? Goddamn—why did I listen to you? I'm starting to think I never needed you in the first place." Then, she swung back around. "I'm going to untie one of your hands, and you're going to draw the mark on my arm. If you mess with me, Cherry, I'll knock your teeth out."

Cherry nodded.

Mai motioned to Owen, who untied one of Cherry's arms.

Cherry took the pen from Mai, her hand shaking, and drew the symbol, the one from her dreams, on Mai's forearm. "There you go. I know how to draw Ziggy, too. Want that? Maybe a pentagram or super S?"

Mai ran her hand softly over the glyph, as if it were a living thing. "I don't know how I could have forgotten what it looked like." Mai turned to Owen and barked, "Get to work."

Owen grinned and pulled out a short black utility knife and Bic lighter from his pocket. "This might hurt a bit."

Cherry panicked. "We had a deal!"

"Calm down," said Mai. "It's not for you."

Owen sparked the lighter and held the flame beneath the blade, and when it had been properly heated, he traced the symbol, cutting into Mai's flesh. She breathed fast, grinding her teeth. Blood trickled down her arm and onto the cement floor.

Cherry winced. "Why now, Mai? Why after all this time?"

"I didn't understand why I wasn't able to do what I wanted to do," said Mai. "But the more I studied, and the more I used the book, the more it became clear: something was missing. All of the pages of the book were still there, so it had to be something else. Then I remembered the photograph—there was something written on the back." Mai nodded to her arm. "This is the key. This…this is how I bring him home."

When Owen finished carving the symbol into her skin, Mai did a little dance.

"Should I give it a try?"

Owen shook his head. "Not here. Not with those cancelling marks on the wall. I suppose you can cross them out, but then you'll have the big guy back at it."

Cherry perked up and looked at the mark on the wall. She needed to figure out a way to get rid of those glyphs.

"Let's go have some fun." When they reached the top of the stairs, the overhead light clicked off.

Mai yelled down, "Sit tight, babe. We'll be back later for a chat. Oh, want me to pick you up anything from the restaurant? On second thought, I think Ramon might be going out of business." The door snapped shut.

Cherry was alone in the pitch-black basement. She tried to rock back and forth to free herself, but it was no use; the ropes were too tight, and the throne weighed a ton.

Cherry felt fifteen again; helpless, alone. For years since her Alternates had arrived she'd hoped for solitude, time to sort out the disaster of a life she'd inherited, but now that her Alternates were no longer with her she wanted them back. Desperately. She wanted Uncle's concern and exasperation, Daisy's optimism and compassion, and Elwood's comfort and strength. She wanted their guidance. Their proximity.

Cherry shouted for Daisy, but there was no response.

She shouted for Elwood. Nothing.

There was only oppressive silence and a hopeful—yet equally terrifying, question— was her crew something more than a coping mechanism? There was only one possible answer.

Yes. They were.

MAMA?

ncle cut the cake, applying a little
too much pressure, mashing a slice
with his ham-fist. Elwood licked
the bottom of the candles, frosting
covering his whiskers and mouth.

Daisy pointed to the thickest slice of cake—for
such a little thing, she always went big. Cherry
leaned back in her chair and laughed. She couldn't
remember a time in her life when she'd been so
content. But why had she been unsatisfied, anyway?
She couldn't remember that. She shrugged.

Uncle slid a slice of cake over and winked
at Cherry, who nodded thank you, but as she
watched the big man serve Elwood, she noticed
that the eye he'd used to wink at her didn't reopen;
it was in a perpetual state of winking.

Cherry leaned forward, waiting for Uncle to
reopen his eye.

"What's wrong?" said Uncle.

Cherry pointed to his eye.

Uncle nodded and smiled as the room around
them started to fall away, revealing statues of men
and women with the heads of cats, snakes, and
hawks.

"Oh, my peeper?" he said. "Gone now. Look—"
He spread his eyelids apart with his thick fingers—
the birthday candles shot out of Elwood's hands
and into the gaping socket. Soon, everything in
the room started to spin and swirl through the

air. A black hole appeared in Uncle's eye socket, sucking everything into the dark cavity.

Cherry hung onto the table, but she felt her grasp loosening.

A frosting-faced Daisy shouted, "Wake up, Mama!"

When Cherry opened her eyes, it was pitch black. She tried to reach out, but she was tied to something. A chair? No. A throne. She was still in Owen's basement—Mai's basement. Still alone. She cried out for Uncle and Elwood, but there was only silence.

In an attempt to calm herself down, she steadied her breathing—they wouldn't just leave her to die, would they? But would this death be any worse than how her dad died? She thought back to that night, seeing it play out against the darkness of the basement as if it were some hellish movie-house with a black velvet curtain. There she was, young Cherry, just fifteen years old, running down the street toward the glow of the Sequoia apartment buildings. But who was that emerging from the lot, the book tucked securely beneath their arm? She hadn't remembered before, but now...now she could see her face clearly. It was Mai.

Then, the scene changed: Cherry was inside the apartment at the Sequoia, orange tongues licking the white walls brown and black. She ran through the apartment calling for her dad. She found him on the floor, a dark circle expanding and soaking into the shag carpet beneath him. He was holding his belly with one hand, but in the other hand was a photograph.

Her younger self ran to her dad's side and tried to drag him out of the apartment, but it was no use—she wasn't strong enough to move him.

"Take this," her dad said, holding out a photograph.

She shook her head, looking for some way to get him out of the apartment.

"Take it!" he shouted. "Read the back."

Even in the intense heat of the burning apartment, the photograph felt damp in her hands. Tears fell from Cherry's eyes onto the picture. She knew the photograph. It was the one that fell out of the book. It was her mom. She flipped the picture over. The firelight made it look as if the symbol was alive. Gold flourishes danced and swirled, the eye on top of the glyph watched her—judged her. She felt a surge of electricity.

"Read it," her dad said again.

Cherry didn't understand—it wasn't a word. How was she supposed to read it? Sirens blared outside of the apartment. "Dad, you're going to be okay. They're going to get you out of here!"

"Cherry, read the name—now! It's important."

"It's a symbol not a word!"

"It's a name."

"How do I read it?" But then, the symbol twisted and morphed into a word. Cherry didn't know how, but she recognized it. She could read it. It was a name. As she spoke it, her dad screamed in agony as he was taken by the flames.

Cherry fell to the ground, disoriented. Broken. The photograph, still clutched in her hand, it began to melt and twist in on itself.

She gasped for air, inhaling all of it: her dad's burning flesh, the ash and fumes from the burnt photograph, the symbol, evaporated tears— the fire! She shouted for help. She called out for someone to save her—anyone.

The black curtain rippled, the movie in Cherry's mind warbled and a new image appeared. There was a face at the door of the apartment, peeking in. And a long, fuzzy white ear. It was Elwood. He hopped through the black smoke and flames and scooped her up off the floor where she lay coughing and sobbing.

And something Cherry hadn't remembered— hadn't seen? There was Uncle, holding up a piece of the ceiling that was coming down so that Elwood could carry her out. And Daisy—sweet Daisy— holding Cherry's hand, telling her everything was going to be okay.

Then the movie in her mind melted away, and she was left alone, crying in the dark on the golden throne.

Cherry shook her head; she'd been cruel to Daisy. She deserved to die in this basement alone for the way she had treated her little friend. And that's what she was, a friend. Her only friends. Her family. Gone.

"I need you, Daisy," she whispered.

A sound from upstairs. The clack of the door opening. Cherry was silent, listening. There was just enough light spilling through the crack in the door to cast a large shadow.

Uncle? she thought.

"Mama?"

"Daisy?" Cherry sat up in her chair. "Daisy? How?"

"Are you okay?" Her small voice was cool water on the flames of Cherry's mind.

"How are you able to be here?"

"Hmm, I don't know. I was…nowhere, and then I was in this house. Where's Uncle and Elwood?"

"Same place you were, I'm guessing."

Upstairs, Daisy opened and closed doors, looking for Uncle and Elwood.

"They're not up here. I'm bored—can we play?"

Cherry laughed. "Sure, Dayz—we can play. But first, there are marks on the wall down here, they're keeping Uncle and Elwood away. I need to figure out how to get rid of them."

"Can I color while I wait?"

"Do you have crayons?" Cherry moved her hand side to side, trying to loosen the rope. Her wrists stung, but she needed to find a way out.

"No," said Daisy. "But there's paint. It's in Mai's bag."

Cherry stopped struggling. "Mai left her bag?"

"Yep! There's blue and green…oh! Maybe I can paint an ocean!"

"Listen, Dayz?"

"Yes?"

"First off, don't you dare paint an ocean—I'm not looking to go swimming at the moment. Listen, we're going to do some art together. Does that sound fun?"

"Yes! But…I can't come down. When I try, it hurts."

Stomp. Stomp. Stomp.

"Daisy? Dayz?"

"Yes, Mama?"

"Can you please stop jumping around for a moment. It's hard to think."

The hopping stopped, and almost immediately, Cherry felt the loneliness set back in; the silence was too much. "Actually, keep jumping—I like to know you're still there."

"Yay!"

Stomp. Stomp. Stomp.

"Daisy? When you said it hurt…how badly?"

"Pretty bad, Mama. Why?"

Cherry shook her head. "Never mind."

Daisy stopped jumping. "Mama?"

"Yes, Daisy?"

"What if I painted over the marks? Would Uncle and Elwood come back?"

Cherry craned her neck to look back at the wall. The marks glowed, pulsating in the low light. "I don't know."

"Well, I can try. Let's use…yellow! There's a bottle of yellow paint!" Daisy came to the door. "Maybe if I do it really fast, it won't hurt as bad."

Cherry rolled her wrists beneath the braided rope—she didn't want Daisy in pain, but what other choice did she have? "Be quick, Dayz. And if it becomes too painful, turn around and run back upstairs. You got that?"

"Yes. Okay. Here I go." Daisy came running down the stairs, her small brown legs moving as fast as they could. She began to cry, then she was screaming—her sweet face twisted in agony as she fell before Cherry on her throne.

"Mama!" cried Daisy. "Mama, help me! Please!"

Cherry tried to move, but it was no use. She screamed for help. She cried.

Daisy began to morph, her angelic face now hideous, suffering, and unfamiliar.

"Daisy! You need to throw the paint on the wall! Do it, now!"

But Daisy couldn't. She was writhing, crying out for Cherry. "Mama, please! I don't want to leave you!"

Inside her, Cherry felt a thousand suns burning hot—she didn't want Daisy to leave, either. She didn't want to be alone. "Daisy, I need you! Throw the paint on the wall, now!"

Daisy crawled toward the symbol, the bottle of paint loosely gripped in her tiny brown hand. Then she stopped moving.

"Daisy..." Cherry whispered. "Daisy, please... please don't leave me."

Daisy lifted her little brown hand and brought it down as hard as she could, right onto the side of the bottle—yellow paint spurted out, and all over the wall, covering the glyphs. Uncle and Elwood fizzled into existence.

Elwood ran over to Daisy, who was already regaining her strength, and held her head in his arms like a distraught mother.

Uncle ran to Cherry. "I'm sorry, Cherry. I would never have left you if—"

"I don't care, Uncle. I only care that you're back with me. I missed you."

Uncle stepped back. "You missed us? Wow, somethin' really bad must have happened for you to have missed us."

Cherry's eyes filled with tears. She wanted to embrace the big lug, but she was still tied to the throne, and she'd never been able to interact with them in that way before. Like the time she tripped getting off the bus downtown; Elwood had tried to catch her as she fell, but when he put his hands out, it was like she'd fallen through a cloud on her way down to the asphalt. But hadn't Daisy picked up the paint bottle? Opened the door?

"Now, now—no tears, Cupcake. We'll figure out a way to get you out of this mess. Maybe we can—"

"Untie me, Uncle."

"Untie you? I can't untie you. We're not...real or whatever."

"Untie me," Cherry repeated.

Uncle looked down at the thick rope and Cherry's raw, pink wrists, and with his thumb and index finger, hooked the rope, and pulled. It snapped as if it were a piece of string.

"Now the other," Cherry said, her eyes ablaze.

"You are real, Uncle. You all are."

Uncle's eyes were wide, his mouth agape. He plucked the rope tied to Cherry's left arm like a bass guitar string. It flew through the air and onto Elwood's head.

Daisy laughed.

Cherry stood, rubbing her wrists. She embraced Uncle, who kept his hands out and to the side, unsure what to do with this affection, then, deciding he liked it, squeezed Cherry back.

"Ouch!" shouted Cherry, laughing.

"Sorry! This was my first hug."

Cherry ran over and embraced Elwood, then lifted Daisy to her feet. "You're the bravest little girl I know. Well, you're the only little girl I know, but still."

"It was scary." Daisy's lip quivered.

"I bet." Cherry pulled her close once more, then stood. "Now, let's get out of here. Mai mentioned something about Ramon, and I want to make sure he's okay."

Uncle hoisted Daisy up onto Elwood's back and then headed for the stairs. "Let's do this."

As Cherry and her Alternates came out through the front door of the brownstone, they stopped dead in their tracks. Lightning lit up stormy gray skies, and blood rained down, coating everything in crimson, filling the air with a metallic odor that reminded Cherry of the jar of pennies her dad used to keep on top of the refrigerator.

"Eff…"

REAL ONES

CHAPTER TWENTY

y the time Cherry and her Alternates got to Black Garlic, they were drenched in blood. Luckily, anyone who happened to be out on the street since the blood rain started falling looked about the same. The sign out front of the restaurant was gone and the windows were shuttered. It looked as if the restaurant had been closed down for years. It made no sense.

Cherry pushed open the door and gasped. Boxes, paint cans, and old bottles littered the floor. In the corner, a table—her table. The table she'd sit at every time she came to Black Garlic.

Elwood's nose wiggled as he sniffed the air.

Cherry walked tentatively through the restaurant toward the back room. "Ramon?"

Uncle pointed to the wall. "Cher, look."

Cherry stopped. Painted across the filthy wall was a glyph that looked a lot like the ones Mai had drawn in the basement of the house on Cedar Street. But this mark reminded her of her friend Ramon. It looked like a man with a towel draped across his shoulder. A slash down the center.

Why would there be a cancelling mark here? Did Mai know we'd escape?

But this mark wasn't meant for Uncle. Nor was it

meant for Daisy or Elwood.

"Mama?" Daisy asked, walking up beside her.

Cherry shook her head and thought back over the past few years. "None of it was real? Ramon… the restaurant. I made it up?"

Uncle picked up a bottle and threw it against the mark on the wall, where it shattered, startling Cherry out of her daze.

"It's real, Cupcake. You made it up, but that don't mean it ain't real. We're real, and we love you. Ramon loved you, too."

Uncle was right. If some of this was real, then all of it was. Cherry took a piece of the glass from the floor and tried to scrape the mark from the wall, but Ramon didn't reappear like her Alternates had. He was gone.

"Why isn't it working?"

Elwood pointed to his forearm.

Cherry understood. She wiped the soot from a chair—her chair—and plopped down. "Because she's got the symbol and the book now. So as long as she's out there willing this shit, it's going to stick? Well, just when I think I'm out, they pull—"

"What do we do now?" said Daisy, climbing into her lap.

Cherry looked at Uncle leaning against the wall, then to Elwood standing near the front kiosk. "Let's decide together. We can leave the City. If we do, maybe we never hear from Mai or Owen again. Or we can go after them."

Daisy looked into Cherry's eyes, then kissed her

cheek. "I'll go wherever you go, Mama."

Elwood nodded in agreement with Daisy.

Uncle looked concerned. "What'll we do if we find them?"

"I don't know, Uncle. I really don't. But we need to get Ramon back, somehow."

Uncle strolled over to Cherry and put his large hand on her shoulder. "This ain't your fault. You know this, right?"

"Not directly, but if Mai was telling the truth about—"

Uncle interrupted, "We can't trust—"

"If she was telling the truth, then Dad started this mess. And I don't know how or why, but Mai thinks my mom is her mom, too." Cherry stood and sat Daisy down in the chair. "I'm not pulling rank. I know that I can, but I'm no longer convinced you're just my broken brain."

Elwood walked over and stood beside Cherry. Daisy did the same.

Uncle shook his head, but smiled. "Sayin' we have a choice while being all noble. You're a natural leader, kid. Lead on, Patton."

Cherry took and squeezed the big man's hand. "Let's get one thing straight, I'm more of a Joan of Arc than a Patton—hell, I'll probably end up burned at the stake."

The broken glass crunched beneath their feet as they stepped outside. Blood continued to fall from the sky, but the sound of thunder was replaced by explosions in the distance. From an apartment window a radio blared reassurance that everything was fine: "President Clinton has been briefed on the red substance falling from the sky, which scientists now believe to be blood. It's not yet apparent where this blood comes from, but experts believe it could be from a nearby slaughterhouse that…what's that, Janet? It's human? Well, developing story here, folks. It appears the blood is human. Health experts are asking people to remain indoors for the time being."

Cherry looked at Uncle. "I'm guessing she went that way."

Daisy splashed in a puddle of blood.

CHAPTER TWENTY-ONE

LET'S PLAY RABBITS AND SNAKES

ngry dark clouds roiled above
Cherry and her Alternates. They
reminded Cherry of the black smoke
the last night she saw her dad. But
she shook her head—there was no time
to indulge in the tragedy of her life.
There was a real threat, and not just
to her and her crew. The entire City
was in a panic; cars sped by, people
ran down the street screaming, and in
the distance something was heading
their way making an awful lot of noise.

Daisy covered her ears. "What's that sound? It's
hurting my ears."

"Whatever it is," Uncle shouted, "it's on its way.
It ain't too late to turn around."

Cherry shook her head and wiped the blood
from her face. "I'm feeling oddly capable of taking
on whatever this might be."

In the distance, a stone snake the size of a three
City buses slithered up and over cars, snatching
people from the street with its large, granite
mouth, popping them between its jaws like paint-
filled balloons.

"Eff," said Cherry. "Ya know, I'm suddenly
feeling a little less capable."

Elwood stepped in front, shoulder to shoulder
with Uncle.

Cherry took a deep breath and then pulled up beside Elwood. She tried to steady her breath, but there was no subduing the fright building within her. She wanted to run in the opposite direction with everyone else. Then, Daisy walked over and leaned against her arm.

"One time," said Daisy, "when you were sleeping, I watched a show on TV about snakes."

"That right?" Cherry looked down at Daisy's big brown eyes and smiled softly. "You learn anything useful?"

"Well," replied Daisy. "I know they don't like strong smells. Oh, do we have garlic?"

Uncle laughed, "I think we'd need a whole lot of garlic."

"Hmm," said Daisy. "Do we know where we can find a big ol' bird?"

The stone serpent caught sight of Cherry and her Alternates, hissed, and slithered through the street, knocking vehicles to the side. Cars and trucks honked, smashing into one another in the chaos. The snake's granite skin moved in waves, pushing it along the pavement, causing an unsettling rasp.

"Let me have first crack," growled Uncle. "I'm an expert knot tier."

"Have at it, big man," Cherry said. "But don't forget, you're not my imagination. This thing might actually be able to hurt you."

Elwood swung Daisy up and onto his back. "Let's play rabbits and snakes!" she shouted.

"Snakes bite, rabbits kick. Uncle, you're a rabbit! Mama, rabbit!"

"Yes," replied Cherry, "I get it—we're all rabbits and the snake monster is a—"

The serpent shot out, its mouth wide enough that Cherry could see the remains of a man whose head rolled out from between polished stone fangs and onto the pavement before her. She dove behind a parked truck just in time, the creature's powerful jaws snapping in the place she'd just been standing.

"Cher, stay outta this!" shouted Uncle, hefting the serpent's tail, and pulling it back.

The creature turned, hissing at the muscle man's audacity.

Elwood jumped from between two parked cars, landing on the snake's unyielding stomach. Daisy squealed with pleasure. "Points for rabbits!"

But then the snake whipped around, sending the rabbit man and Daisy sprawling onto the asphalt.

"Ouch! That's not nice!" said Daisy, scowling.

Cherry picked up a metal pipe from a damaged shop front and ran at the serpent, while Uncle jumped up and onto the creature's neck, prying its jaw back with his giant, callused hands. "Say ahh!"

As the creature fell to the ground, writhing in pain, Cherry ran up and jammed the pipe into its mouth. A moment later it bent the metal in half as if it were a stick of gum.

The serpent shook its granite head, throwing Uncle to the ground, scattering several garbage cans like bowling pins.

Daisy ran over to Cherry and hid behind her leg. "What do we do?"

It was no use; the creature was too powerful. But how could it exist out here on the street? There were no glyphs painted across the City. None that Cherry could see.

She watched as the serpent twisted up Elwood with its body, while Uncle tried to pry him free. *Think, Cherry. Think.* Then it hit her—the symbol Owen had carved into Mai's arm was the key to all of this. And maybe, just maybe, it was part of her.

Cherry closed her eyes. "I want this blood rain to stop."

She opened her eyes; the rain was still coming down. What was she doing? In a moment, the granite serpent would crush Uncle and Elwood, and she was here making childish wishes.

No. She had no time for wishing. She closed her eyes once more.

"This blood rain stops now!"

Daisy ran over and tugged on Cherry's blouse. "Mama, it stopped! It's not raining red anymore!"

Cherry opened her eyes and gasped. "Holy shit." She stepped out and into the street. "Hey, you!"

The serpent turned its stone head toward Cherry and the cowering little girl.

"There's a giant, snake-eating eagle heading your way!"

From somewhere up above, there was a screech.

The serpent looked to the sky, loosening its grip on Elwood.

Uncle grabbed his rabbit friend and carted him off to the side of the road.

It was silent. The cars stopped honking and revving; everyone looked to the sky. Dark clouds gathered, morphing, wisps becoming feathers, and billowy gray buffs becoming talons and a beak, until the cloud was the shape of a majestic bird. It descended like a meteor, slamming into the body of the snake, shaking the earth below, then it ascended back into the sky, the stone serpent dangling from its stormy talons, until it was out of sight.

Uncle and Elwood ran over. "Christ on a cracker," said Uncle out of breath. "What was that?"

"I told you! Eagles!" Daisy hopped on one leg, laughing. "But you probably could have wished for garlic."

"It wasn't a wish...not exactly. It was a command. I—I'm not sure what's going on, but I think whatever it is that Mai has...I think I've got it, too." Cherry picked up Daisy and set her on top of Elwood's shoulders. "I'm guessing we're heading in the right direction. Look, in the sky over there."

In the distance the sky opened, sunlight beaming

down to the tops of the buildings below.

Uncle strutted down the street toward the sounds of chaos, rolling his shoulders. *"Andiamo—* let's do this."

IT'S HARD TO PRONOUNCE

CHAPTER TWENTY-TWO

herry and her Alternates followed the serpent's trail of destruction.

Elwood twitched his nose and nodded to steps leading up to a large building.

"The City Museum," said Cherry. "Haven't been here since…well, since before Dad died."

It was eerily quiet. The typical bustling downtown was desolate. On the stone steps leading up to the museum a security guard's limp body was being torn apart by cats made of gold. They watched Cherry and her Alternates slide past to the door of the building through emerald eyes. They were definitely on the right track.

"Mama, is he okay?" asked Daisy, peeking out from between Elwood's fuzzy ears.

"No, honey. He's not."

In the lobby it was just as quiet, the only sounds echoing from Cherry's boots walking across the marble floor.

"Where are they?" asked Uncle, looking down a darkened hallway. "Maybe they didn't come this way."

Cherry shook her head. "Listen."

A muffled shout sounded from somewhere within the building.

Cherry looked at her Alternates. Why was she here risking their lives? She could leave now, get out of the City, maybe head to Portland or Seattle. It wasn't her job to save anyone but her friends and herself. But wasn't Ramon her friend, too?

Elwood approached, wiggling his nose.

"Elwood, is this dumb?" Cherry stroked his long, soft ear. "You're all trying to protect me, and I'm forcing us into a dangerous situation because… because what? Because of my shitty parents?"

Elwood removed Daisy from his shoulders, took Cherry and Daisy's hands, and then nodded to Uncle.

"We ain't got time for this, Bugs," said Uncle, looking around cautiously.

Elwood nodded again, and then stomped his giant white foot to show he was serious.

"Alright, alright." Uncle took Cherry and Daisy's hands, and together, the four of them formed a circle. "You going to say some words, Elwood?"

Elwood shook his head and nodded to Daisy.

"Um…" said Daisy with a giggle. "Rub-a-dub-dub, thanks for the grub?"

Elwood shook his head impatiently.

Uncle rolled his eyes.

"Um…oh! I know! Mama, I think Elwood wants me to tell you that we're with you no matter what. We want what you want."

Elwood nodded once in confirmation.

Cherry shook her head. "But what if I don't know what it is I want? What if I'm too mixed up to deal with this world? What if…what if I'm too broken to make a good decision, like ever?"

Uncle squeezed Cherry's hand. "Cupcake, the *world* is broken, and right now, you might be the only thing holdin' it all together. You've already made your decision, and it's the right one. Besides, whatever happened to you that night at the motel, during the fire, it's given you some sort of…somethin'. You conjured an eagle for Christ's sake. I'm not scared. Not for me, not for Daisy or Elwood, and certainly not for you. In fact, I'm feeling damn good about this."

Cherry laughed, pulled her Alternates in for a hug, wiped the tears from her eyes, and said, "Let's do this for Ramon. I'm betting they've gone there." Cherry pointed to a banner.

Daisy read aloud, "Experience the…"

"Ancient," Uncle helped out.

Daisy continued, "The *ancient* power of Isis. Who is Isis?"

"A goddess," said Cherry. "Dad and I used to come here when I was younger—this exhibit has been around since forever. You know, Isis is one of the reasons I got so into *Cleopatra*. I remember a funny story Dad used to tell me about Isis. See, she started collecting Ra's drool when they went out for walks."

Daisy laughed. "Drool? Eww!"

"Who is Ra?" asked Uncle.

"He was the sun god. Like, super duper powerful. And Isis wanted that power—that's why she collected the drool. Isis made a serpent out of the drool—what a freak, right?"

Cherry and her Alternates started walking toward the exhibit.

Uncle shook his head. "Why the serpent?"

"She created it so that it would bite Ra."

"I don't get it," said Uncle.

Cherry rolled her eyes. "I'm getting to it. Isis offered to heal Ra, but only if he gave her his secret name—the name being the key to unlimited power." Cherry stopped walking. *Unlimited power.*

Daisy climbed up Elwood's back and onto his shoulders. "What was his name, Mama?"

Cherry's eyes were wide. She thought of the symbol. The name. "It's hard to pronounce, Dayz."

FAMILY

CHAPTER TWENTY-THREE

When Cherry and her Alternates found Mai, she was standing at the center of the spacious, dimly-lit room which housed the Isis exhibit. She was frantically thumbing through the pages of the book, muttering something indistinguishable beneath her breath.

On top of Mai's head was a regal gold crown in the shape of a vulture. Its ruby eyes glinted beneath a spotlight and its gilded wings extended well below her ears; it looked as if at any moment it might fly off her head. Cherry recognized the crown of Isis at once. She'd last seen it when she was with her dad, over eight years ago. The sight sent a shooting pang of grief through her body.

On either side of Mai, two sentinels with faces painted onto smooth sandstone and wearing *shendyts* stood with their hands on their hips.

Uncle nodded toward Owen, whose body was in the corner of the room among a trio of stone vessels. His face was gone; his eyes, nose, and mouth were hidden beneath thick folds of pink flesh with terrible gouges raked into them. At first Cherry thought an animal had got to him, but Owen's fingers were bloody. He'd tried to claw the skin off.

Elwood hopped to one side of the room with Daisy bouncing up and down on his back, as if she were riding a camel through the desert. Uncle circled to the other side of the hall.

"Mai," Cherry called, but Mai didn't look up. "Mai," she shouted again.

Mai slowly lifted her head. "You should go."

"I'll go after I'm sure you're not going to hurt anyone else." Cherry stepped forward.

"What makes you think I'd hurt anyone? I'm trying to save my dad—so leave. Now!" Mai looked down at the book and shook her head. "It's not working…but it will."

"You can't save your dad, Mai. Your dad died seven years ago, just like mine. You're hurting people—you killed Owen."

Mai shrugged. "He was way too into that band Live. That one song, over and over again. There's not a jury in the world would convict me. That part about the placenta falling to the floor? What was that all about?"

"Please. You have to stop this."

Mai shook her head. "I didn't mean for anyone to die—honestly. But shit happens, as they say. And so here we are. I'm going to let you go, Cher Bear. I'm going to let you walk right out of here with your little crew—so just go."

"We're not leaving, Mai. Not until you hand over the book and—"

"Hand over the book to you? You're delusional. I'm going to figure out how to bring my dad back, and then, together, him and I will set everything right."

"Let's talk, Mai," said Cherry, trying to make her voice calm despite the thrumming in her chest. "The photograph—the one with the glyph on the back—you said that was your mom?"

Mai looked up at Cherry with sad eyes. "She was beautiful. Wasn't she?"

"I guess that makes us sisters?"

Mai narrowed her eyes. "What are you talking about?"

"I'm not joking—that's my mom," said Cherry. "Her name was Eset. My dad met her in Egypt—he lived there for a year before I was born. I was young when she left us, but dad kept her picture framed beside his bed. He never got over her. Something tells me your dad never really got over her, either."

Mai closed the book and stared at Cherry without speaking.

Cherry continued, "So if anyone can relate to you, it's me. And yeah, Mai, I would love to hug my dad one last time, but he's dead. We get one life and that's it. It's hard to let people go but—"

"Why would I let him go if I don't have to? Are you really saying you would pass up the opportunity to have him back. If we really are half-sisters…then let's bring them back, together. We'll all walk out of here one big weird family."

Daisy made a sound. Mai looked over at her.

"Something funny about that?" said Mai.

Daisy nodded. "Cherry already has a weird family."

"Mai," said Cherry. "Our dads are dead, and that's something we need to accept, because that's part of life. It's the other side of the same coin, you know? If you would have asked me to join you in this—resurrection—the night he died in the fire, I would have jumped at the chance. But I've been grieving him too long to stop now. His death is part of who I've become, and to tell you the truth, I sort of like the current version of myself."

"Well I don't like me," said Mai. "And I don't like you, either. It's all fucked. But I'm going to unfuck it, because I can. I have the power to—"

"If you had the power to bring your dad back, you would have by now."

Mai shook her head and opened the book again. "I just need to figure it out. Must be a combination, the book and the glyph, you know? To bring people back from the dead. I'm missing something or—"

Uncle dove at Mai, but just before he could swat the book from her hands, one of the stone men stepped in front of him, slamming him to the marble below, which splintered like a cracked egg.

"Son of a—" Before Uncle could finish his sentence, he was being swung by one of his thick legs in circles, and thrown against the wall.

Elwood took Daisy from his shoulders and set her down on top of a small platform next to a statue of a limestone crocodile with the head of a hawk. Then he hopped higher than Cherry had ever seen him hop before and came down right onto Mai. The book flew from her hands, sliding across the floor, a few feet from Cherry, who picked it up and dusted it off.

The stone man ran toward Cherry, its face cold and expressionless. It lifted its fist. Cherry shouted, "Freeze!" The stone man froze, his sandstone hand still raised above his head.

Daisy clapped. "Good job, Mama!"

Across the room, Uncle was dislodging himself from the wall and getting to his feet. He shook out his hair, which was almost completely white from the sheetrock.

"It's over, Mai," said Cherry. "I've got the book."

Mai limped over to the large tinted window and looked out onto the street at the chaos left behind by the stone snake and blood rain. "It doesn't work that way, Cher Bear," she said. "I've got the glyph—I can conjure at will now. So give me back my book so I can bring Dad home, or I'm going to kill you—sister or not." Mai paused, then looked back at Cherry. "How did you get out of the basement, anyway?"

"This needs to end right now, Mai."

"Oh, I agree, babe." Mai whispered something under her breath. "I've been trying to think of what would really bum you out right now. Like, what's the one thing you're most afraid of? It sort of just hit me—fire."

Uncle moved in front of Cherry. Elwood did the same.

A cracking sound came from the platform where Daisy stood, and a moment later the hawk-headed crocodile statue slithered off its base and down to the floor.

Daisy jumped out of the way and screamed.

The creature waited like an attack dog for the word, staring at Uncle, Elwood, and Cherry. Mai narrowed her eyes and stepped forward. At the back of the room, the doors slammed shut, sealing them in. Then, all around the room, fire erupted. Flames roared and climbed the walls.

Cherry looked around wildly as the fire consumed the walls and ate at the display cases filled with artifacts. Her legs buckled and she began to hyperventilate. The ground was cool on her palms but the heat from the fire pressed against her scalp and face. She screamed—she needed to get out of this place.

Breathe, she thought. *Breathe through it.*

The hawk-headed crocodile darted at Cherry.

Uncle ran full speed at the stone reptile and grabbed it by its tail, flinging it to the opposite side of the room where it crashed into a burning display case, smashing the wood and glass into a thousand pieces.

"Touch the pussy and you're gonna get fucked!" he shouted.

Cherry steadied her breath and nodded at Uncle approvingly just before the second stone man came out of nowhere and grabbed her by her throat.

The room grew dark, and in her mind, Cherry saw her dad's face just before the fire consumed him; he looked peaceful. She felt that same peace. Death wasn't so bad. No more fear. No failure. No more sadness. She opened her eyes. She wanted one last look before she went away from this terrible place. The stone man's stoic face was frightening, but in just a moment, it would be gone. In just a moment, the world would be—

The stone man's head shattered into a million pieces. Dust and rubble rained down over its shoulders, falling to the marble floors below. Behind him, where his head was only moments before, was Uncle. His ham fist was full of dust.

The stone hand released Cherry, who fell to the floor, gasping for air. She wasn't dead, and that felt pretty good. Seeing Uncle's face felt pretty damn good, too. Elwood jumped onto the back of the limestone crocodile as it ran back into the fray, but it was too powerful, throwing him to the ground with ease. It stalked them, hissing, rasping its beak across the marble floor from side to side, sharpening it.

Daisy snatched the book from the floor.

Cherry could barely swallow, but she shouted as loud as she could, "Daisy, throw it into the fire!"

Daisy wound up to throw the book into the flames, but it was too late; Mai pushed her to the ground. The book slid across the marble floor— Mai ran toward it.

Cherry got there first. She held the book to her chest and shouted, "The book is on fire!"

The book erupted in flames, consuming the

pages and the cover as if it were soaked in lighter fluid. Smoke and flames engulfed Cherry—she screamed.

Mai reached through the flames, but quickly retracted her arm, crying out in pain.

A black cloud of smoke surrounded Cherry, burning her throat as she gasped for air. She felt her face sag and blister. But she didn't let go. She thought of her dad—a flawed man, not unlike Mai's father. She thought of poor Ramon and the restaurant, a casualty of Mai's grief and hatred. But what kept her from letting go of the book was her Alternates. They were her family, and she needed to keep them safe. She loved them. And they loved her. Through the cyclone of black exhaust, a child's hand touched Cherry's face. Daisy stepped through the smoke and wrapped her arms around her. Then there was Uncle and Elwood. They wrapped her up so tight that the flames couldn't breathe. The pain was smothered. The sadness, whatever remained from the past seven years of grief, smothered.

The smoke cleared as the book fell to ashes at their feet.

The stone hawk-headed crocodile stopped moving, no longer filled with life, and sprinklers came on. The flames slowly shrunk, leaving behind a design of char peaks and valleys across the walls of the room, until all of the flames were finally extinguished.

Mai whispered something to herself, then

looked around the room. Nothing happened. She screamed it, "The water stops! The room is on fire! Cherry is dead! She's dead! Dead! Dead! Dead!"

Nothing. Mai's arm was burned, the glyph carved into her skin mangled in twisted flesh.

Cherry raised her hand to her face, expecting to feel raw flesh come off in her fingers, but she wasn't burned at all. She spoke, "The sprinklers are off."

The sprinkler system shut off.

Mai looked up at Cherry and shook her head. "How?"

"I don't know, Mai. It's a part of me. I've denied it for a long time, but the book, the symbol, the power—it's all part of me."

"You can do it, Cherry," pleaded Mai. "You can bring them both back. If we're sisters—and I know that we are now. You'd do this for me. Please. Please do this for me, Cherry. I just want my dad back."

Cherry shook her head. "I'm sorry, Mai. Even if I were able to, which I don't think I can, because I've wished and prayed for him back enough times to know it ain't happening, I wouldn't do it now. We get one life and that's it."

Mai's eyes darkened. "So what now?"

"I don't know. I guess you'll need to own up to killing Owen and all of those people out on the street?"

Mai shook her head. "No, I don't think so. I think it's more likely that Owen did all this."

"But—"

"But what? What can you possibly tell the police to make them think I'm responsible for all this?" Mai smirked. "Where's your proof, babe?"

Daisy took Cherry by the hand. "Mama, we should go."

Cherry looked at Mai for several moments, then said, "I need a way out."

A door appeared at the back of the room, where once there was none. Cherry and her Alternates walked through it, but before they left, Cherry turned, and added, "Mai wrote a letter confessing to the murder of Owen. It's on her nightstand at her house."

Mai turned red, removed the vulture crown from her head, and kicked it across the room.

Cherry took the cigarette from behind her ear and smelled it, then she let it hang from the corner of her mouth, just like her dad used to. "Peace out, babe."

* * * FAMILY * * *

CHAPTER TWENTY-FOUR

WASTE NO WISH

ack at her apartment, there was one thing they needed to take care of right away.

"Please be careful, Uncle. The last thing we need is to have that thing land on somebody out walking their pooch."

Uncle balanced the television set, which teetered on the edge of the windowsill.

Daisy squeezed in beside him. "Clear!"

"Bombs away!" he shouted, and a moment later the television smashed on the sidewalk below. A woman waiting at a bus stop across the street looked up to the window where Uncle and Daisy were peering down at the destruction below, but to her there was nobody there.

Daisy grabbed Uncle by his massive mitts and spun him around in circles, laughing at the sour expression on his face.

Elwood hopped over to Cherry, who sat on the couch, and nuzzled her.

"What now, Cupcake?" said Uncle in mid-spin.

"I guess I'll need to find a job."

Daisy chimed in, "Can't you just wish for money?"

It began to rain outside. Cherry looked at Uncle and raised an eyebrow.

"Don't worry—it ain't blood."

Cherry exhaled, then said, "Well, Dayz, I suppose I could wish for money, but that's such a boring thing to waste a wish on."

"How about some lunch, Boss?" called a familiar voice from the kitchen.

"What would I do without you, Ramon?" Cherry smiled. It felt good to have her friend back.

"Somethin' I don't get," said Uncle.

Cherry looked up at Uncle. "What's that?"

"How you two got the same mom."

"Well," said Cherry, "I remember Dad talking about his life in Egypt before I came along. He loved it there. Met my mom in the lobby of a hotel. He said she was the most beautiful woman in the world. I'm not sure how Mai's dad met her, but I'm guessing they met her around the same time, maybe even through Dad. Maybe we should visit Mai and ask her how her dad and mom met?"

"She killed your dad," said Uncle.

"Sure, but my dad has some responsibility in her dad's death, too. Besides, I know what grief can do to a person. But for now, why don't we just enjoy a meal together and figure out what we're going to do now that we're not fighting for our lives."

Daisy jumped up and down and shouted, "Let's play squids and whales!"

Cherry looked at her Alternates, playing and laughing together. They were her friends. Her family. She didn't need the book or a secret name. She didn't need power. She had everything she needed right here.

A lot goes into writing a book, and it starts long before even a single drop of ink is spilled. It starts with love, hopefully. It starts with pain and loss and failure, likely. It starts with pleasure, divinity, and sin—a whole lot of sinnin', definitely! Then, when you're coated in all that gooey, sparkly liminal dust—the debris of life's triumphs and tribulations—that's when you're ready to sit down and write a story. So to everyone in my past—angel, devil, and those in between—I thank you from the bottom of my malformed heart.

Special thank you to my early readers, EJ Trask, J. Curtis, Jessica Maison, JR Phillips, and my dope-ass wife, Tricia Bitter.

Cherry Kills was edited by S.E. Reid.

Cover art by Butcher Billy.

Book design by Shane Bzdok.

Published through the mighty Tiny Worlds. Thank you, J. Curtis!

Sean Thomas McDonnell is a contest-winning Bay Area author specializing in horror and dark speculative fiction. His debut collection, *Beneath the Valley Oak*—a fierce blend of western grit and creeping dread—sold out within 48 hours. He is a founding creator of *The Midnight Vault* anthology and the author of the standout story *Blink Twice If You Can Hear Me*. He writes regularly on his Substack, Automatic Writer.

automaticwriter.substack.com

www.ingramcontent.com/pod-product-compliance
Lightning Source LLC
Chambersburg PA
CBHW031133130726
47988CB00006B/2347